BITTER MELODY

by

Loretta Jackson and Vickie Britton

Loretta Jackson Vickie Britton
1-26-06

WHISKEY CREEK PRESS
www.whiskeycreekpress.com

Published by
WHISKEY CREEK PRESS

P.O. Box 726
Lusk, Wyoming 82225
307-334-3165
www.whiskeycreekpress.com

Names, characters and incidents depicted in this book are products of the author's imagination or are used fictitiously. Any resemblance to actual events, locales, organizations, or persons, living or dead, is entirely coincidental and beyond the intent of the author or the publisher.

ISBN 1-59374-122-7

Printed in the United States of America

Dedication

To our cousin and traveling companion, Darlyne Standley

Chapter One

Amid the buzz of excited talk and laughter, Elaine waited tensely for the audition to continue. She felt a thrill of excitement as the man in charge strode center-stage to survey the crowd.

Again, she marveled at how striking the famous country singer of the Wind River Band appeared in person. Rex Tobin's muscular build in Western shirt, well-fitting denims and dark boots, gave him a natural, unaffected appearance.

Coal black hair, thick and ruffled, added an appealing element of ruggedness the magazines and even TV cameras had failed to capture. For an instant his piercing blue eyes locked on Elaine and she felt a catch in her breath.

Rex Tobin's lingering gaze, the reassuring warmth of his smile, seemed momentarily just for her. Was he about to call her name? Elaine's stomach tied in knots as she waited. "Next on the list," he said, "Derrick Klein."

Feeling dizzy with relief, Elaine glanced toward her companion. Everyone always thought of them as a pair, although Derrick and she considered themselves only friends. When Derrick had learned about today's auditions at Craft Music Productions, of course he had wanted to try out too. She watched as Derrick made his slow, easy way toward the stage.

With languid confidence, he paused to smooth his hair. His shoulders hunched as he leaned his tall frame closer to the microphone. His voice carried a ring of nonchalance that Elaine had always before considered appealing. As she listened now, she wasn't so sure.

Elaine tried to take her mind off the fact that she would probably be next, wondering for the thousandth time at her friend's apparent lack of nervousness. She knew that, when her turn came, she would stand on stage feeling as though her body were held together by tightly stretched wires. But she wouldn't think of that now.

She concentrated, instead, on Derrick. Usually she admired his abundant ease, but today this characteristic seemed twice magnified, and instead of working in his favor seemed to mark him as an amateur. Elaine knew she didn't even qualify for that label. She had almost no experience singing before an audience!

Her father's death, three months ago, had brought chaos and financial ruin to her. Although she was a songwriter, not a singer, the stacks of medical bills, the pressure of increasing debt, had prompted her to sign up for the audition.

Derrick's second selection had ended. He smiled, ducked his head lazily, and left the microphone. Elaine stole a glance at Rex Tobin, who now stood on the outskirts of the stage next to a distinguished man with silver hair. She thought she read some negative decision in his smoky blue eyes before he glanced at the paper in his hand and called out, “Elaine Sands.”

Elaine rose; so tense she was unable to even smile in answer to Derrick's wink as he passed her. Panic suddenly seized her. What was she doing here? She belonged back at the desk in her room, content to work alone, unnoticed, lost in notes and verses. To calm her nervousness, she took a deep breath. She would give this her best try. After all, she was the daughter of the great writer and singer, S.S. Sands.

“I would like to do one of my own songs,” she said into the microphone.

She turned anxiously to the three backup musicians up on the stage who, with instruments ready, waited.

“I am changing the order of the numbers I gave you, if you don't mind. I want to do the second selection first.”

The youngest band member had begun tuning his guitar and the man beside him, a tall, brawny red-head, gave no acknowledgement that they had even heard her. But the third musician, a big, middle-aged man, who played the steel guitar, smiled and nodded.

“I like that one best, too.”

His fingers moved expertly over the strings as he spoke.

Before Elaine turned back to the crowd, she glimpsed her own image in the chrome stand in front of the mike. Her thick, dark blonde hair looked disheveled. Locks of it clung to her damp forehead. Her tanned skin contrasted with her light eyes and white dress. Elaine started to sing, but the microphone was too high. She hadn't thought to adjust it. Her mouth felt dry and she couldn't keep the tension from her voice. Finishing this song was going to take a good deal of courage.

She could see Derrick, slumped in his chair, fingers under his chin, nodding approval. Derrick seemed oblivious to the fact that things had gone wrong for him, that they were going wrong for her. She had made a grave mistake coming here today. After this was over, Derrick and she would stop by The Highlands, her cousin's club, have dinner and laugh about this pathetic attempt to join such a well-known tour.

Freed for a moment, she felt as if her performance was improving. Her gaze wandered to Rex Tobin, whose eyes never left her face. Was it approval she saw in his intent expression, or rejection? The youngest band member, long-haired and sullen, had set aside his guitar and moved over to the drums. Suddenly distracted, flustered by both the abrupt change and by Rex Tobin's unyielding gaze, Elaine's voice faltered. Quickly, she recovered her pace. But something was dreadfully wrong.

She hadn't written the song to be played with such a loud beat. The music began at once to over-power her lyrics and destroy the message she had worked so hard to perfect. No matter how hard she tried, she couldn't bring back the haunting, melancholy strains which had caused the song to work.

"You didn't love me yesterday, and I won't love you tomorrow." Even though the song was about to end, not being able to bear it any longer, Elaine raised her hand for the musicians to stop playing.

"I need to start again," she said, facing the pleasant man she had spoken to earlier. "Would you please change to my other selection?"

At that moment Rex Tobin stepped out on the stage. He glanced at his watch.

"I'm afraid we don't have time for any more." Then to the audience, "We will resume auditioning at one o'clock."

Even though Rex Tobin sounded polite and apologetic, Elaine, reacting to the pressure of the moment, felt his interruption rude, and responded with a flare of anger. Elaine had intended to challenge him, but he had already turned away to address the silver-haired man, who had followed him to the center of the platform. She directed her words to the steel-guitar player.

"Why can't I at least finish one song?"

The big man let his hand play absently across the strings.

"I just hang around the throne," he answered dolefully. "I'm not the king."

Elaine steeled herself as she strode forward to confront Rex Tobin.

"Mr. Tobin," she said, "I'll ask you. Can I talk to you directly, or do I have to send a courier?"

Rex's blue eyes, lit with the sparkle of a smile, caught her off guard. As she faced him defiantly, an electric awareness stirred through her. She had been unprepared for the endless depths of Rex Tobin's eyes, so dark blue they seemed to merge with the black pupils.

"I spent a great deal of time preparing for this audition. You could at least allow me to complete my songs."

A gentleness mixed with the strength of his features, as if he fully understood and sympathized. She had expected him to respond to her remark with annoyance, but instead he spoke softly.

"I have only one observation. All the others auditioned because they enjoy singing."

Straightening a little as she spoke, Elaine said, "Music is everything to me!"

"But how serious are you about conveying your message to an audience?"

No use trying to explain to him that she aspired only to write songs, not sing them, that only the great need for money had forced her to audition for him in the first place.

"I sang just as seriously as you listened!"

Elaine could hear the sharp click of her high heels on the wooden stage floor as she hurried down the steps and started up the steep, inclining auditorium. She felt the eyes of the few that remained following her as she hurried past vast rows of seats. She would soon be outside, far away from the burning humiliation, away from Rex Tobin!

"Wait a minute, Miss..."

"Sands," the older man supplied for him.

"Miss Sands."

BITTER MELODY

Jackson / Britton

Elaine stopped walking and watched Rex Tobin stride quickly down the long aisle. His blue-black eyes left her feeling hypnotized, unable to look away. In spite of herself, Elaine felt her anger diminishing.

"Don't misunderstand me. I would be the first to admit that you have much potential."

The deep voice, edged with sincerity, soothed her injured pride and made her feel undeniably drawn to him. How could she be so overwhelming attracted to someone she had just met?

"In fact, I was greatly impressed by the haunting quality of your voice. I think you could be a real success, with a willingness to work hard and make many sacrifices. Most people lack the intestinal fortitude to do that."

"Don't concern yourself with my fortitude," Elaine answered. "I will always put music first in my life!"

Elaine started for the door.

"Miss Sands," Rex Tobin's deep voice called her back. "Don't leave. I think you might be exactly what I'm looking for."

Elaine turned back to him slowly.

"I should never have auditioned for your show," she told him frankly. "I am a songwriter, not a singer. I have almost no experience performing before a large audience."

"Experience you can gain. All you need is opportunity." He studied her carefully for a moment. "There is a temporary spot on the show for a female singer that must be filled immediately. If you are interested, Miss Sands, I'm willing to take a chance on you."

Elaine's heartbeat quickened. Before she could respond, clouds of doubt overshadowed her elation. As if sensing Elaine's hesitation, Rex added quickly, “Before you make a final decision, why don't you join our practice session here tomorrow afternoon? In fact, let's meet a little early so I can fill you in on some details. Would you be free to have lunch with me next door at Renaldo’s at one o'clock?”

CHAPTER TWO

How many other women had held their breaths as they had gazed into Rex Tobin's wonderfully blue eyes, Elaine wondered as she sat across from Derrick that evening at The Highlands, the dinner club owned by her older cousin, Thad.

Had Rex Tobin made a decision to hire her because he really believed she had talent and the determination to succeed? Or had he felt the same physical attraction as she, and had not wanted her to walk out of his life?

She found herself only half-listening to Derrick's rambling talk. The great joy she had felt when she had accepted Rex's invitation for lunch tomorrow had become tarnished with doubts. Elaine agonized over how little she knew about him. Rex Tobin was one of those private celebrities who shunned reporters and being in the news. Still, from time to time, his name had been linked with up-and-coming stars, such as the beautiful Lisa Craft.

Elaine had sudden misgivings about her good fortune. She might be better off if she had not read the ad cousin Thad had shown her, had not listened to his encouragement to try out for the audition. Still, it wouldn't hurt to meet Rex tomorrow, as promised. She wasn't going to join his tour unless she was fully convinced she should do so.

"This is no way to celebrate!" Derrick grinned. "Let's blow the budget and order Thad's specialty."

Derrick called to a waitress, "Throw a couple of your best steaks on the grill!"

Elaine was relieved that Derrick was not disappointed that Rex Tobin wanted to hire her, but not him. She had somehow expected the evening to be a difficult one, filled with periods of his brooding silences. Elaine's gaze flitted across a worn curtain that hung at the sides of a huge, center stage, then across the marred, wooden tables occupied by men and women wearing blue jeans and faded shirts, their faces either very hard or very weary.

Once The Highlands, opulent and successful, had been swamped with promising, young stars on the rise. That was when her father, S.S. Sands, had drawn in the crowds. Now it seemed only a slightly shoddy hangout for the ever-hopefuls.

"I picked out *our* favorite spot tonight," Derrick said, "where Thad first introduced us. We've composed some good songs together, right here at this very table!"

Besides her own stock of songs, Elaine and Derrick had collaborated on a small collection. If she started touring, they would not be able to write any more music together, yet Derrick's voice held no suggestion of sadness.

Their food soon arrived. Elaine tried hard to relax. Her eyes wandered again toward the worn stage. Her first singing appearance had been here in this very room—her first failure. Because her father was too ill to do his show, she had sung his opening solo, "Danny Boy." She had become confused, stumbled over the words, lost the melody, and had at age thirteen received rounds of laughter.

Elaine still rankled from the demeaning shame she had felt. Both her cousin and Dad had done their best to comfort her. "Very few singers can master that song," Thad had told her. But no amount of consolation had eased her sense of personal tragedy. She had vowed she would never sing on stage again, and had not except for those occasional duets with Derrick. What had ever possessed her to try out for a popular show where she would be constantly in the public eye? As if aware of her doubts, Derrick raised his mug of coffee.

"To success," he said, "to a rising star!"

Forcing her gaze away from the stage, Elaine waved to her cousin, Thad, who was coming over to join them. Thad, the only relative she had left, spent his spare time promoting music. His office was crammed with tapes of would-be singers and song writers, for whom he acted as agent. That, along with owning and operating this club, forced him to keep up a tremendous pace. Elaine was probably the only one who knew that he was often hard-pressed and unhappy.

The Highlands had once been spotlessly clean and well-lit, but had recently grown to look more like the dark waterfront hangouts that surrounded it. A large portion of ceiling, stained from a leaking roof, made it look even more run-down. Elaine could not bear seeing Thad's club in this poor condition, on the verge of collapse—a magnificent failure, just as Thad himself often looked. If she accepted the job Rex Tobin offered, she would be able to help Thad renovate.

She smiled at her cousin as he approached, studying the craggy face, slightly hooked nose, the deep-set brown eyes that in contrast with his light skin and blonde hair gave him the appearance of a river-boat gambler. His fondness for silk shirts and shimmering vests added a final touch of flair.

"She made it!" Derrick called, a big, easy smile spreading across his face. "Elaine Sands! Star of the Rex Tobin Show!"

"Elaine, honey, I am so proud of you!" Delight danced in Thad's brown eyes. "What a wonderful break! When I was your age, I would have given anything for a chance like you're being handed!"

Speculative lines deepened in Thad's hollow face. "Why am I getting the impression that I am happier about this than you are?"

"Because you are," Derrick answered for Elaine as Thad sat down. "Elaine is having second thoughts about leaving New Orleans behind. And me."

Elaine studied Derrick, dreading the jealousy she knew would eventually surface. Had he sensed her attraction to Rex?

"I've heard lots of conflicting stories about this Rex Tobin." Concern gave a touch of edginess to Thad's voice.

"Derrick, what's your impression of him? What's he like?"

"The question is not what he's like, but what he *likes*!

"I'll tell you this much, Thad, this big-shot Tobin was very much impressed with Elaine."

In a half-joking manner, Thad suggested, "Maybe you ought to tag along, then, and look after her."

"You know what I'm thinking, Honey?"

Derrick turned his most appealing gaze upon Elaine. "I'm thinking he would find a place for me on his show, if you asked him to."

* * * *

Lively sounds of guitar and piano drifted up to the bare rooms above The Highlands that most of her life Elaine had called home. It would continue, she knew, until one or two in the morning. Her drab, studio apartment looked shadowy and empty. She had recently sold the best items of furniture to pay bills. Now even that stock of money was hopelessly depleted. No matter what qualms she had, she needed this job!

Elaine thought of Thad, downstairs, who seemed to work day and night. Even after Dad had gotten too sick to sing, Thad had managed to sell enough of his old songs to keep them going. Thad bragged about being personally acquainted with major publishers and producers on Music Row in Nashville, but Elaine realized his connections consisted mostly of making phone calls that weren't returned and sending demo tapes that were seldom even played.

Dad should have tried to sell his songs himself, but

loyal to his nephew, Dad had continued to allow Thad to market all of his work—except that one large file Elaine now took from the cabinet and carried with her to the table. This special collection of music he had selected and saved to record himself, his best work, yet un-reviewed, unheard.

Elaine opened the folder where Dad had written, "The Louisiana Drifter" by S.S. Sands. She skimmed the song titles—"Dreamspell," "Little Blue Heron," "Moonlit Darling." then she lifted what she considered the best song Dad had ever written, "Silver Bayou Dreamer."

Why did he have to die so young?

"I've had a good life, Elaine." These were his last words before the operation he didn't live through. A good life—snatches of it replayed though Elaine's mind. She thought of the dim places where he sang for so little money, of the dreams that he held on to through endless disappointments, of the years of ego-smashing rejections, eased a little by Thad's unwavering optimism.

Dad had encouraged Elaine to be a teacher, to go into the retail sales business, to turn to any profession but music. No doubt other occupations paid a steady and satisfying wage, but somehow they were not for her. Her inheritance, intangible, but very valuable and very real, was her plan to follow in her father's footsteps, and she knew already what sacrifices awaited.

Elaine's eyes fell back to the paper.

"Silver Bayou dreamer, Hide away from life.
Live alone in shadows, For love is only strife."

BITTER MELODY

Jackson / Britton

Although the words were simple, the music had an undercurrent of complexity that engaged the heart. Now that he was gone, the rights to all of S.S. Sand's songs belonged to Elaine. Why not do what she could to keep his memory alive? She did indeed have something to offer the Rex Tobin show—Father's compositions and her own! Elaine would take this song tomorrow. Her reservations lifted as she thought of the handsome man with those smoky eyes that she felt able to read the contents of her heart.

CHAPTER THREE

Early the next morning Elaine chose her best dress in pale yellow silk with loose, flowing skirt, to wear for her luncheon date with Rex Tobin. The small, intimate restaurant was dwarfed by the imposing building of tinted glass where she had auditioned yesterday. Arriving early, Elaine seated herself so she could see the swinging doors through which Rex would pass.

She told the waiter to return later for her order. After a long time she checked her watch—already one-thirty. Had Rex Tobin simply forgotten? Elaine gazed from the window again, then around the cozy restaurant with its clean white linen and hanging plants. Her mood of excitement became streaked with hurt. Rex Tobin had been constantly on her mind since their eyes had first met. Obviously he had not thought about her at all.

A cultured voice broke into her thoughts. "Sorry I'm late."

The silver-haired man who had stood beside Rex at the audition slipped into the seat beside her. He looked, Elaine thought, dignified and sophisticated, like a Roman senator who had traded his toga for an expensive Western-style suit. "Mr. Tobin is unable to keep his appointment and asked me to fill in. I'm Levi Culver."

Taking off dark-tinted glasses, he reached for the menu. "Do you like Cajun food?"

"I'll just have something light," Elaine said, trying to hide her disappointment.

"Things have been hectic at Craft Music Productions," Levi explained after they had ordered. Then he added as if trying in his polite way to supply excuse for Rex Tobin, "As you probably know, the music business is filled with unexpected interruptions."

Elaine attempted to smile as if Rex's absence did not matter to her. She should never have allowed herself to read so much in Rex's impulsive decision, in his deep, intimate gaze.

The food came, a seafood salad for Elaine, shrimp in red, spicy sauce for Levi.

"Did you ever meet Bill Craft, the founder of our company?" Levi asked.

"No, but my cousin Thad knew him."

"You're more likely to have heard of Bill's daughter, well, adopted daughter, Lisa."

"Everyone's heard of Lisa Craft," Elaine admitted, an image from the tabloids filling her mind, a dark-haired beauty in glittering dress being escorted to some social function upon Rex Tobin's arm.

"Bill passed away recently," Levi said. "Before he died, he made Rex a partner in the company. Together, he and

Lisa run the business. That's where Rex is now, with Lisa, in conference."

Elaine felt puzzled at the rush of strong feeling that the thought of them together brought.

She asked casually, "Do the two of them get along well?"

"Lisa?" Levi laughed. "She couldn't get along with jolly old St. Nick himself!"

He turned suddenly serious. "Since you're going to be part of our group, you might as well know the whole story. Lisa has no experience in running a company and tends to be extravagant. Bill took Rex in because he didn't want Lisa left alone on the managing end of the business. He wanted her provided for, but he also wanted someone who could actually run Craft Music Productions. What Bill actually hoped is that the two of them would marry, but that hasn't happened...yet."

"Have you worked for Craft Music Productions long?"

"Just since Rex became a part of it. Rex used to work for me at Groves Recording. When Bill offered Rex the partnership, Rex persuaded me to work for him."

"Do you tour with the band?"

"Yes, I sing and also play background music. When we're not on the road, I'm an accountant more than anything else." He paused. "Lisa was scheduled to go on tour with us, but out of the blue she changed her mind. Probably a result of one of her and Rex's fabulous fights. Anyway, that left us with a gap in the show, which Rex has chosen you to fill. We leave this coming Thursday."

Elaine drew in her breath. That wouldn't give her much time to make her decision or to prepare. Levi took a paper from his jacket pocket and spread it on the table.

"We'll be playing first for a centennial celebration in a little town near Evangeline Park. There won't be a big crowd, which will give you a chance to relax and get accustomed to everything before we hit the cities. From there, the two-week tour makes a big circle. Houston—that's the big one—then Corpus Christi, San Antonio, and back to New Orleans for the grand finale." Hotels are reserved and paid for by the company, but your meals are up to you. Everyone generally travels in the tour bus."

After they had eaten, Elaine and Levi crossed over to Craft Music Productions' vast lobby. Two secretaries behind a circular desk in the center answered questions and directed waiting people to upstairs offices. Rex stepped out of the elevator. Beside him, dressed in a smart designer suit of vivid blue, walked a beautiful, dark-haired woman Elaine recognized at once as Lisa Craft.

Rex quickly strode forward and the light that came into his eyes made Elaine forget about the broken lunch date.

"I apologize for not being able to meet you for dinner, but a problem unexpectedly came up. Do you have any questions about the tour?"

"Mr. Culver filled me in on most everything."

"I can always count on Levi."

Rex smiled and drew her toward where Levi now stood talking to Lisa. "Elaine, I would like you to meet Lisa Craft. Lisa is..." he started, but his voice trailed away.

"...Is the cause of my gray hair," Levi finished for him.

Levi looked pleased when his remark drew an approving laugh from Lisa.

Lisa's charcoal hair feathered away from a perfectly sculptured face, dominated by large, violet eyes. Proud and confident, she stood as tall as Levi. She looked so aloof and distant that Elaine was surprised by the warmth in her voice.

"So this is my replacement," she said in an accepting way. "I knew I could count on Rex to find someone *just right*. Welcome to our company, Elaine. This might well be a day we will all remember."

"Your welcome is a little premature," Elaine answered with a smile. "I've made no decision yet about the tour."

"I know it looks as if we're rushing you," Rex said, his hand tightening on Elaine's arm. "But from what I heard, you won't need much time to prepare. Levi will introduce you to the band. I've got some more business to see to, but I will try to join you later."

As Levi and Elaine entered the auditorium, the same big man that had played for her audition sat behind his steel guitar. She had noted already that he was the best musician. It was this man alone who had captured the feeling of her song.

She had immediately liked him, the crinkles about his blue eyes, his kindly manner, slow and humorous. Today he wore blue jeans and a red plaid shirt that fit tightly across an ample stomach. When he saw them approach, he took off a huge, tan Stetson and ran a large hand through a mass of graying hair.

"Big Oscar Macy," Levi introduced. "A one-man show. Singer, musician, clown."

"Mostly clown," a curt voice called from behind the curtain.

Big Oscar gave an exaggerated bow. "I am not the best," he said. "I am the *very* best!"

"He really believes that."

Through the folds of gold curtain, another musician, who had also played at her audition, appeared.

"That's what makes him so utterly sickening."

Even though he spoke pleasantly enough, Elaine detected an undercurrent of genuine dislike.

"I'm Denny Mack," he announced.

His very assertiveness seemed to draw great attention. He all but strutted out to meet them. He was six-foot two, very masculine and fit. His longish hair had sandy tints, but his trim beard was dark red. His slightly up-turned nose and pale skin were sprinkled with freckles.

"I used to have my own show," Denny Mack said.

Oscar strummed his guitar and sang mournfully, "Until they closed him down, and ran him out of town."

Denny started to shoot back a retort, but Levi intercepted.

"Where is Shelby?"

Levi looked around the empty auditorium. "Let's start without him. Denny, you said you needed to work on the music for your first song."

Denny Mack must favor pop music, for Oscar Macy

moved to the piano. Elaine marveled at the expert way Macy could change instruments. When engaged in music, the two men seemed to get along. Big Oscar's jokes and laughter kept the long period of waiting from dragging.

Finally it was her time to sing. Shelby, who looked like a surly adolescent, slipped in half way through her song. Immediately he began beating the drums.

She stopped singing and turned to face him. Elaine had met hundreds of young men just like him, long-haired, sulky, their whole world centered around themselves. She tried to be nice.

"Would it be possible for you to change to the guitar?"

He answered her coldly. "Drums are what I do best."

Denny Mack shot a grin from Shelby to her as if he somehow approved of the boy's stand.

Instead of starting the number again, she took the music for her father's song, "Silver Bayou Dreamer" from her bag and handed it to Oscar Macy.

Oscar studied the sheets with great interest for a while, then he began playing the melody on his guitar. Skillful fingers at once captured the heart of the song. She sang a few lines of lyrics, which increased Oscar's enthusiasm.

"This is going to be the best number on the show!" he exclaimed.

"My father wrote it," she answered proudly.

Oscar passed the music to Levi.

"First class stuff!" he said. "We'd better feature this one!"

"I'll show it to Rex," Levi answered, then to her.

"Now, let's go back to your first song."

The music began again. The drum-beat started as loudly as before. Rex Tobin entered the auditorium. As Elaine sang, Levi left the platform to give Rex Tobin the music for "Silver Bayou Dreamer." She could hear scraps of their conversation, Levi saying, "This is a real find!"

She watched breathlessly as Rex scanned her father's song. Why was he frowning? Surely he would recognize it as the masterpiece it was! Rex, the music tight in his hand, paused to listen to her singing, then called out.

"Shelby, I told you yesterday to go easy on those drums."

Shelby immediately rose. His dark eyes burned as he stared at Rex. But his only answer was the hateful way he snatched up his guitar. After Elaine had completed her number, she walked over to where Rex Tobin stood.

"Do you like the song Levi showed you?" she asked, trying not to sound anxious.

The same odd look appeared on Rex Tobin's face.

"I don't believe it is for this show," he said, not sharply, but gently, as if he had gleaned that this song was special to her.

Elaine's heart sank. Her attempts to keep him from seeing her reaction were not needed, for he did not look at her as he handed back her father's work.

She clutched the rejected sheets tightly. It had not occurred to her that Rex Tobin would not be deeply impressed by "Silver Bayou Dreamer." Disbelief mingled with disappointment.

"I have a meeting," Rex said abruptly, then to Levi. "Just stick with Elaine's original selections."

Rex's rejection caused a tightness in Elaine's throat, a hollow feeling in the pit of her stomach. Levi and Elaine watched Rex's quick exit in silence.

"He doesn't like last minute changes," Levi said apologetically.

Anger rose from the bewilderment Elaine felt. Rex Tobin had not even bothered to meet her for lunch, and now he did not even take seriously the gift of her father's finest work! Her eyes fell to the skillful notes of "Silver Bayou Dreamer." If Rex Tobin didn't like what she could contribute to his show, then she had nothing at all to offer!

"Tell Rex Tobin," she said to Levi, struggling to fight back tears of disappointment, "that I will not be joining the tour."

CHAPTER FOUR

Elaine sat alone at The Highlands in the shadow of the empty stage, grateful for the darkness and the comfort of familiar surroundings. Her career as a songwriter was promising. Right here at this very table she had basked in the glow of success. And here Derrick and she had celebrated the sale of compositions they had worked on together. This, not singing, was her life.

Then why did she feel so gloomy and sad? In her heart she knew it was not the loss of the singing contract, but the fact that she would not be seeing Rex Tobin again.

She lifted the cup to her lips and drank deeply of the strong, bitter coffee. When she looked up, Rex was standing squarely in front of her. His eyes, shaded by the dimness of the club, never-the-less smoldered, causing that confusing intensity of feeling to arise in her again.

"I knew right away, the moment I heard you sing just one line, that you had a rare talent. That's why I hired you," he said, and without invitation he seated himself opposite her. "Don't think for a minute I'm going to let you go now."

Before Elaine could fully recover from the shock of

seeing Rex here, her cousin Thad entered the huge dining area from his side office. He stopped a big smile on his lined face as he headed toward them, extending his hand to Rex. "I never thought I'd see Rex Tobin in my club!" he said exuberantly.

Rex rose.

"Good to see you, Mr. McConnell."

"Drop that Mr. stuff. Just call me Thad."

Elaine, with sinking heart, knew Thad would not budge from the table while Rex remained in the room. Thad turned his fond gaze to her.

"Elaine's father, S.S. Sands, sang here all the time!" he bragged, indicating a picture from the line of them that stretched across the south wall.

"I didn't know S.S. Sands was your father," Rex answered politely. "He has always been one of my favorites."

"Would you do me a special favor?" Thad asked. "Sing one of your songs for us. Then I can tell everyone Rex Tobin was right here on my stage!"

"Thad," Elaine started to protest, "don't..."

But Rex seemed pleased by the request.

"I'd be honored."

He slipped off his jacket and left it on the chair beside her. Lights suddenly flooded the stage. Rex lifted a guitar and switched on the microphone.

"I'm going to sing this song for Elaine Sands," he announced, drawing the attention of the few late diners seated among empty tables.

The brilliant, overhead lights caused ripples in his thick, black hair and reflected in his deep blue eyes. The song he had selected, Elaine had not heard before. For a while only guitar strings sounded, played in a style all his own, one that changed from slow and soothing to dramatic and intense. Elaine watched his strong hands, his muscular arms, bare and tanned. The deep emotion expressed in his words sent a thrill through her.

"I close my eyes and think I dreamed you, girl I've searched for all my life."

Had the dedication been only a polite gesture on his part, or had he carefully chosen this particular song especially for her? She listened in a dream-like way, aware of his deep voice, his lingering gaze, and for a brief interval she allowed herself to believe that he had. When the song ended, still under the spell of his music, she watched Rex return to their table. Thad, now standing, applauded long after the others had stopped.

Rex took from the pocket of his jacket a contract and a check for a thousand dollars and placed them in front of her.

"An advance," he said.

Elaine hesitated, conscious of Rex willing her to sign. Eagerly Thad supplied a pen from his breast pocket. Elaine looked from Thad to Rex and slowly drawing in her breath, wrote her name on the line beneath Rex's.

When she had finished the signature, she looked up to see Derrick, looking angered and hurt, standing in the doorway. How long had he been watching them? Startled by the strange, tight set of his features, she waved for him to join them. Instead Derrick turned and stalked out.

"I wonder..." she began.

Rex's eyes seemed to darken as he waited for her to speak.

"At the audition," she started again, "do you remember hearing Derrick Klein?"

Rex hesitated.

"Yes."

"Derrick and I..."

"All the positions for the show are filled," Rex cut in, as if to spare her the process of asking.

"But would you just listen to him again? He is very talented."

Rex's reply was terse, abrupt.

"I'm sorry. I'm afraid there is no place in my show for him."

* * * *

The unexpected advance seemed an answer to a prayer. Elaine was free until tomorrow morning when she would meet and practice with the Wind River Band, so today would be a good time to go shopping. The prospect of helping Elaine select her wardrobe elated Thad, who had an eye for style and flare.

He took her to the best stores and waited, craggy face tilted to the side, brown eyes critical of every modeling.

"Doesn't fit right," he complained about her first selection. "Too much glitz and glamour," he commented about the second. The third he simply brushed away with a wave of his hand.

By four o'clock Elaine was still without purchases and getting desperate.

"I have one more place in mind," Thad insisted with a gust of his inexhaustible energy. "Over at the west end there's a little shop with styles right from Paris. Originals."

"I didn't get a million dollar advance, Thad."

"Don't you worry," he said with a wink. "I know Sandy. We'll work out some deal with her."

The owner of the shop, an attractive brunette who seemed to have fallen prey to Thad's charms, hurried to display her most expensive gowns. Elaine dared not even look at the price tags.

Elaine selected a dress of deep gold with the same highlights as her hair and soon stepped from the dressing room to the large, curving mirrors.

Elaine could see Thad's reflection behind her in the glass, nodding approval. "That's a keeper. Now, try on the one I like."

The moment Elaine slipped on the stunning gown of deep sapphire mingled with shimmering silver; she knew it was just right. The waist, long and clinging, accentuated her slim curves.

"Perfect!" Thad exclaimed the moment she appeared before him. "You look just like an angel. In this dress, the one that old Thad picked you, you're going to bring down the house!"

Darkness had begun to fall by the time they returned to The Highlands. Happy from her shopping spree, she hadn't thought of Derrick until she entered the club and found him missing from his usual place at the front-row table. Derrick and she had been good friends for such a long time; she felt saddened by his absence. She would have liked to explain to him that she had really wanted him on the show, enough even, to ask Rex to reconsider.

When Derrick didn't show up, she went up to her room and for a while sat by the window where she could see the front parking lot and hear the laughter and voices of people who entered and left. The shrill ringing of the phone caused her to start. Rex Tobin flitted though her mind as she reached for the receiver with anticipation.

"Elaine Sands."

She waited for a few seconds that seemed much longer to her, but no one spoke. She said hello again and repeated her name. A slow, throaty voice, barely above a whisper, answered. She strained to make out the words.

"If you join Rex Tobin's tour, you will be *very, very sorry."*

"What? Who is this?"

Elaine couldn't tell whether the voice was male or female, yet she couldn't mistake the low, certain threat that it clearly conveyed. She waited a while longer, knowing that whoever had spoken was also waiting.

"Who is this?" she repeated, her voice, this time filled with alarm.

A click sounded on the other end of the line.

Did Derrick want her to stay badly enough to make such a foolish phone call? She knew that after she left the club in the evenings, Derrick sometimes drank more than he should, but whoever had made the call had sounded sober and deadly serious.

Only a few people would know of her plans—Rex Tobin and his band and whomever they had told, but she could surely eliminate them. Thad was overjoyed at the thought of her touring with the Rex Tobin show. This call must be some sort of a sick joke.

Woodenly Elaine turned from the phone. The room, darkened and drab, added to the looming sense she had of some impending disaster.

Morning and sunlight made her put aside the phone call as a mere prank. She went downstairs, spotting Derrick. Large, hazel eyes turned soberly to her as she approached.

"So you'll be leaving tomorrow," he said, as if this were something he no longer wanted her to do.

Elaine thought of the long hours the two of them had spent composing their songs. She saw their occasional co-writing team beginning to crumble and said, "I've only signed with him for this one, short tour."

She had really wanted Derrick on the show, but not entirely for his sake. Night after night at The Highlands they had sung their songs to one another and in recent years the only times she had performed on stage in front of an audience was to accompany Derrick in a duet. The transition from writer to singer would be much easier with Derrick beside her.

"I asked Rex Tobin about hiring you," she said. "But all the positions for the tour are taken. Maybe...later on."

"He's never going to hire me."

"Derrick, would you see me off tomorrow? Please."

Derrick stood up and turned away from her. She could see only his tense back and his thin shoulders.

"You don't need me," he answered coldly.

CHAPTER FIVE

Elaine drew in a breath of excitement as her eyes fastened upon the words *Rex Tobin and the Wind River Band* so impressively emblazoned in silver upon the side of the waiting bus. Thad had risen early to see her off. Rex, as if he had been watching for her arrival, stepped out of the cab and met them at the car.

His hand, warm and strong, covered hers. "Welcome," he said.

"All aboard!"

Oscar Macy, brimming with cheerful good nature hurried forward to take Elaine's guitar and luggage.

"I'll be helping Levi with the driving," Rex said. "Oscar will show you around the bus."

Elaine said goodbye to Thad and once more glanced around anxiously, hoping to catch sight of Derrick's old Buick. She remembered the bitterness in his voice last night, and wished their parting had not been on such strained terms. As she entered the bus, she looked back to where Thad still waited. When he saw her, he gave one last, enthusiastic wave.

Qualms, which had been increasing since she had received the warning phone call, became an active fear. What a mistake she had made by impulsively signing that contract! She did not even want to be a singer. She felt an oppressive dread of her fast-approaching first performance.

From behind a heavy, plastic partition, Elaine could see Levi at the wheel of the bus, Rex in the passenger seat beside him.

"Good morning, Elaine," Levi's voice called through a built-in intercom system. "We'll be leaving in a few minutes."

"Welcome to the castle."

From the small round table, Denny Mack greeted her, his fingers deftly shuffling a pack of cards. His wide, confident smile made brown eyes glisten, accentuated his large, perfect teeth. Again, Elaine was aware of the artificial charisma about him, the too-bright beard that drew the eye, the well-toned physique that surely brought him admiring glances. His boldness created a sort of appeal that Elaine knew would draw in a crowd of followers.

Shelby, the lank-haired boy beside him, raised sullen, dark eyes to her, but did not speak.

"Our child star is furious," Oscar announced. "Rex and he had a fight over his use of drums for your first number. Rex told him he wasn't going to play at all on tonight's show."

Shelby's scowl deepened. Was his grudge at Rex or her, in particular or the world in general?

"I'll give you the grand tour," Oscar spoke again. "Our

little home on the road. Over here is a small kitchen complete with refrigerator, and beyond is a little lounge area with a sofa for naps. Since we stay in hotels, the bus wasn't built for sleeping, but sometimes we do travel late into the night. We don't have an official driver. Levi and Rex do most of the chauffeuring, but all of us take a turn at the wheel."

Elaine followed Big Oscar Macy's large steps as he moved toward the back of the spacious, blue-carpeted bus. In the far corner sat lifting bars and weights.

"Denny and Shelby are on some kind of health kick." Loudly, so that Denny would be sure to hear, he added, "Even Denny's brains are beginning to bulge with muscles."

Denny retorted, "And that spare tire you're carrying around with you will come in handy in case we have a flat!"

Smiling, Oscar parted a curtain to show Elaine a little dressing room. "There's a place back here to stash your clothing," he said, handing her the garment bag. "The dresses hanging here are Lisa's."

Elaine felt a rocking motion and steadied herself as the bus turned and began to pull out on to the highway.

"You just get settled in," Oscar said, then he added in a much louder tone, "I have to get back to the cards before Denny stacks that deck."

Elaine felt a tight ball of tension in her stomach as she hung up and carefully smoothed her clothes. Tonight, she would wear the deep gold, she decided, and save the special blue and silver one Thad swore made her look like an angel for the big show in Houston.

She lingered, her attention caught by Lisa's gowns, one of glittering, brilliant green, another, a gold-sequined scarlet. Elaine's dresses beside such vivid colors seemed to lose all luster. If Lisa and Rex hadn't fought, if Lisa hadn't dropped this tour, Elaine wouldn't even be here. She was, after all, only Lisa Craft's last minute replacement.

Elaine wondered once more about the cool, dark-haired beauty's relationship with Rex. She recalled with a pang of disappointment how Rex had canceled his lunch date with her to meet with Lisa. Were they, as Levi had hinted, more than just business partners?

Gradually becoming accustomed to the constant motion of the bus, Elaine arranged her guitar and suitcase, then retuned with her writing pad to join the others. She seated herself in an empty seat near the window, opposite the small table where the three had resumed their card game.

"Want us to deal you in?" Oscar asked.

She appreciated his trying to put her at ease. She did feel a little awkward, the only woman on the bus.

"No, thanks. I'll just do a little writing."

"If you hang around with us long enough, you'll have to play poker," Denny Mack insisted.

"Women never make good poker players," Shelby said, shaking back his dark hair in a practiced gesture of insolence.

Elaine could not have been raised anywhere near Thad McConnell and not acquired skill at playing poker. She should just show the impudent Shelby how wrong he was.

Resisting the temptation, Elaine settled into a seat and watched the scenery pass by the window. The bus was crossing the endless length of bridge across Lake Pontchartrain. The sky looked overcast, as gray and uneasy as the water below.

The unsettled weather made her think again, though she tried not to, of the ominous phone call, and she felt a small shiver of apprehension. What if it hadn't just been some absurd joke?

The heavy city traffic thinned and soon they turned on a narrow road that would eventually lead them to Evangeline Park. They should reach the little town of Delta long before dusk. At least this first performance would not be in some vast concert hall! Again, she felt stirrings of anxiety. Even though rehearsal had gone well enough, always in the back of her mind was the fear that she might once again fail, experience a repeat of her vivid childhood memory, that choked, panicked feeling that made a jumbled mess of music to a song she had known all her life.

Elaine focused her attention to the words she had carefully written in her notebook. The lyrics were beginning to develop into another sad, parting-of-the-ways, love ballad. Nothing she would ever write would compare with "Silver Bayou Dreamer." Deep inside she had expected Rex to feel the same way about her father's songs as she did. What else about him would turn out to disillusion her?

"You should listen to your uncle," Oscar Macy was saying to Shelby. "His taking you along this summer is an advantage you're too young and dumb to even appreciate.

Why, when I was your age, I would have given my right arm for a chance to travel with a *real* band."

"I didn't ask to come along on this tour! I want to play my own kind of music, not his!"

"Come right down to it," Oscar drawled, "there's only two kinds of music—good music and bad music."

"Don't be putting Shelby down," Denny cut in curtly. "This boy's the best drummer around. The mighty Rex Tobin isn't always right, in case you don't know that."

Denny's contempt for Rex, a contempt tinged with jealousy, filled his words as he went on. "Rex Tobin wants to be the star, to make everyone else, including me, take a back seat. The kid here is top of the line. If this were my show..."

"It's not your show, Denny." Oscar replied. "No one said Shelby wasn't talented, but he has to learn not to throw us all off beat. How does he expect Elaine to sing with that bongo-playing drowning out her voice?"

Shelby turned to glare at Elaine. In a lower tone, that he probably didn't think she could hear, he added resentfully, "If it wasn't for her, I'd be going on tonight, not setting up the stupid equipment!"

"When you learn to work with us, not against us, Rex will be glad to let you play on stage."

With a defiant toss of long hair, Shelby slammed down his cards and stalked off to the back of the bus. Denny followed him.

Elaine continued writing to the methodical thumping of weights. Once she glanced up to see Oscar alone at the table, absently shuffling cards, dealing out a single hand of solitaire.

"Can you play double solitaire?" Elaine asked, putting aside her work to slide into the empty seat across the table.

Oscar began to deal her some cards.

"In the end," he said with a sad smile, "We all find ourselves playing solo."

Elaine had felt an immediate liking for the big, joking man, who could capture with a few strums of his guitar the spirit of a song. Shelby's storming off had upset him, and she didn't like to see him in this hurt and injured mood.

"That boy sometimes just gets under my skin," Oscar said. "Rex took on a handful when he took him on this summer."

"Maybe Shelby's not as tough as he seems."

"He's been in all kinds of trouble. His mother kicked him out. If it weren't for Rex, he wouldn't even have a place to live."

For the first time, Elaine felt the undercurrents of tension that existed between the members of the band. Oscar and she played round after round of double solitaire while Denny and Shelby kept to themselves in the back.

The bus finally pulled to a halt at a city park on the outskirts of some small town. Anxious for a breath of fresh air, Elaine stepped outside. She felt the humidity heavy in the air and noticed the clouds overhead, bulging with unspent rain.

"There hasn't been a restaurant for miles," Elaine heard Levi say.

"There's a picnic table," Oscar said, striding toward them. "Now all we lack is a picnic."

He pointed to a building across the street.

"See that blue sign? It looks like a convenience store. I'll just wander over there and bring us back a bite to eat."

"We haven't passed a decent-sized town since we left New Orleans," Levi complained. He looked down at his fancy, patent-leather boots. "I hate this back-woods country."

"Levi's idea of a decent-sized town is half a million," Rex said and smiled.

"I'll admit I'm a city slicker," Levi confessed, "accustomed to the finer things in life."

He glanced overhead with a grimace, "And we would have an outdoor gig scheduled for tonight. Do you think we'll have to cancel, Rex?"

"Not unless it gets worse," Rex answered. "We'll just have to wait and see."

Oscar soon returned lugging a large paper sack. "We're in luck."

He began to set food on the table—a less than glamorous lunch—of bologna, bread and cheese, chocolate milk and pineapple rolls with thick icing.

"What are you trying to do, kill us?" Shelby cried out as Oscar lifted the last item from the sack, a tin of sardines.

"What?" Oscar said with a quizzical look. "I thought sardines were supposed to be good for you."

"Look at this stuff, all those fats and starches," Denny said. "I can't eat any of that."

Oscar shrugged, making himself a bologna sandwich. "Suit yourself."

"Come on, Shelby," Denny said, slinging a comradely arm across the boy's shoulder. "We'll just walk over there and buy something fit for human consumption."

Rex helped himself to chocolate milk and a sandwich. Levi and Elaine politely accepted the offered food.

"Disappointed?" Rex asked, joining her at the far end of the picnic table, away from where Oscar and Levi talked.

"I've eaten plenty of meals of bologna and cheese," she responded, remembering the times she had traveled with her father, happy days even though they had often lived on sack lunches and slept in dreary hotels.

"Life on the road isn't all glitz and glamour," he said with that arresting smile that had first drawn her to him. "But when we get into the city, I'll assure you we will stay in style. Big hotels and fancy restaurants. It will be all you ever dreamed."

Just being with him, no matter where they were or what the circumstances, was beginning to be Elaine's dream. She felt the gaze of his deep blue eyes upon her and glanced away, fearful that her expression might give away her thoughts.

Shelby and Denny were returning with cartons of yogurt.

"Oscar told me Shelby is your nephew," she said.

Rex nodded.

"He's been going through a hard time. My brother, Shelby's father, died in a car accident a few years ago. His mother recently remarried. Shelby began hanging around with bad company, getting into all kinds of trouble. So I sort of took him under my wing this summer. He's not a bad kid," Rex continued. His tone of voice gave away his fondness for the boy. "But he lacks discipline. He's always been crazy about music. When he was younger, he looked up to me. I took him along this summer, hoping to get close to him again. But things have changed between us."

"Maybe it will just take some time."

Rex's gaze strayed to where Shelby and Denny stood talking together.

"Everyone needs a hero." His blue eyes darkened with a wistful sadness.

"I guess I was hoping Shelby's role model would be me. But I'll accept Denny, if that's what he wants."

After they had eaten, Rex suggested, "Shall we take a little walk down by the water and stretch our legs?"

Elaine fell into step beside him as they strolled down the winding lane. The trees, heavy with Spanish moss, reflected in the still water and recalled to her the haunting strains of her father's song, "Silver Bayou Dreamer."

"This bayou country," Rex said, as they stopped beneath the shade of a cypress tree, "is a great change from where I grew up."

"Where was that?"

"In Wyoming. Near Wind River Canyon."

Wind River, that's accounted for the name Rex had chosen for his band. "I'm sure it's a lot different from New Orleans."

"Yes. Deep snow and harsh winters, a place where you can drive for miles without seeing a single soul, just rangeland and rough cliffs." Rex, lost in remembrance, smiled. "And the people you meet there are just as strong as the land."

Just like him, rugged and independent. Elaine wished she could mingle with those ranchers, see for herself the twisting canyon land.

As if reading her mind, he said, "Some day I'll take you out there. On my land in Wind River Canyon there's a waterfall. The most beautiful spot on earth."

For the first time that day, Elaine began to feel a sense of relaxation. Being here with Rex, talking with him so easily, put her mind at ease.

"I suppose it's natural for you to be interested in music," Rex commented, "with S.S. Sands for a father."

"Yes, we were very close. My father had so much to give the world. Maybe, if he hadn't died so young..." Elaine's voice trailed off. She was thinking about the collection of his best songs, the ones he had never had a chance to sing.

"My father had such a captivating voice."

"Like yours," Rex said.

"I tried to be honest with you. I've done very little singing before audiences. Just Derrick and I at The Highlands, and that was the two of us together." She hesitated. "I feel very uneasy about tonight."

She saw darkness move into Rex's eyes. "Is that why you wanted me to hire Derrick? As a crutch? A certain nervousness is necessary to a good performance."

"I'm hoping in time to get over it."

"You won't, not entirely. I understand exactly what you're feeling now, Elaine," he said, compassion deepening in his voice. "I still remember my first audition. I didn't get hired. It was six months before I got the courage to sing again."

"I'll give tonight my best try," Elaine said.

"I know you will. And I'll do everything I can to make it easier for you. There's one thing my experience has taught me about stage fright. The best way to deal with it is to jump right in, like plunging into icy water on a hot summer's day."

Rex gave her a long, considering look.

"That's why I'm going to change my plans and let you go on first tonight. I'm going to have you announce us and open the show with your songs."

Elaine had just begun to feel at ease, almost confident about tonight. Now his sudden change in her schedule caused a whole new wave of fears to surface.

"I would rather sing in the same order we practiced," she said.

Rex looked at her steadily. The strong, firm line of his jaw told her that he was not likely to reconsider.

"You'll do just fine, Elaine. As a songwriter, you have great feeling for the lyrics. Just remember, your job is to think about nothing but your message."

Rex smiled at her in that special way. It seemed natural for his arms to slip around her, for his lips to find hers. As they walked back hand in hand to the bus, Elaine felt the first real happiness she had felt in a very long time.

CHAPTER SIX

When the bus arrived in Delta, large droplets of rain were beginning to fall. Last-minute jitters made Elaine ask Oscar hopefully, "Do you think we might have to cancel?"

"We play come rain or shine," Oscar responded.

From the steamed-up bus window they could see the weather beaten pavilion with its wooden timbers and sloping roof, the rain-streaked banner advertising the night's performance of *Rex Tobin and the Wind River Band*.

Their accommodations, a rustic lodge nearby, looked as bleak and forlorn as the rapidly-darkening sky.

"Some hotel," Levi remarked as his gaze raised to the moose head that hung over the stone fireplace in the lobby.

Beyond, Elaine could see a dining room and small, adjoining lounge. Rex took charge.

"Levi, will you see that the equipment is unloaded right away so Shelby can get started setting up?"

He checked his watch.

"The rest of us will meet at the pavilion at eight."

Elaine was too nervous to manage more than a few bites of the sandwich she had ordered from room service, but she was grateful for the steaming pot of tea. Brushing out her thick, honey-colored hair, she gave it an extra spritz of hair spray hoping the style would last despite the dampness. After carefully applying her makeup, she slipped into the satiny golden dress, all the while trying to ignore the fluttering in her stomach.

She glanced in the mirror and saw what might be a stranger's face—a self-confident woman with steady green eyes and an elusive smile. Glad her inner nervousness was not reflected in her image, she hurried downstairs to meet the others. Denny Mack whistled as she descended the steps.

"Isn't she a heart-stopper!"

Oscar, wearing white Stetson and denim suit, looked homey in contrast to Denny's more formal attire. "Let's go!" Oscar signaled to Levi.

Elaine was surprised to see how dark it had grown outside. The brooding atmosphere of Spanish moss and cypress, the thick, rain-laden air made the night seem even darker and more oppressive. As the bus drove the short distance from the hotel to the weathered pavilion, footlights appeared, making the entire area near the stage glow with brilliance.

The band waited in the small room behind the stage area. Like the rest of the building, it had exposed rafters and wide-open windows, where, despite the overhanging roof, water had entered and gathered in recesses on the wooden floor.

A few minutes before the show was scheduled to start,

the rain came pouring down in buckets, clattering against the tin roof, making people huddle inside. A fairly good-sized crowd had gathered, filling the folding chairs beneath the shelter, standing in bare spaces just out of reach of the storm.

Elaine, poised in the doorway, glanced back to see Shelby sullenly adjusting the amplifiers and checking the equipment. Noticing her, he glared. His accusing look told Elaine that he still blamed her for not being allowed to go on tonight. Shelby's glowering look increased her stirrings of uneasiness. Elaine took a deep breath, mentally preparing herself to step out on the stage alone. If only her mouth wasn't so dry!

"Is there somewhere I can get a drink of water?" she asked Levi.

"Back on that table you'll find my Thermos. Lemon juice," he said, "it's good for the throat."

Elaine entered the anteroom where Shelby was working. She poured herself a drink and said to the boy, "Butterflies."

"Don't worry," Shelby responded grudgingly. "You'll make an impression."

He could have at least added *good*, she thought, as she returned to wait near the side curtain. Rex's deep voice sounded from beside her.

"We're going to have a good crowd in spite of the storm."

Elaine turned to face him, noticing how very handsome he looked, damp, black hair contrasting with white shirt.

The black suit added height and leanness to his form.

"Your introduction starts in five minutes," he said, reaching for her hand. "Remember what I told you. Plunge right in. Even icy water is cold only for a while. And, Elaine, concentrate on the words."

Elaine had little time to worry about stage fright. She felt only a moment of doubt when she walked on stage. The informal atmosphere of the rustic, open building, torrents of rain intermingling with the cheerful murmurings of the crowd, made it easier. Elaine forced herself to look out into the audience. Suddenly, to her surprise, she spotted a familiar face. Derrick, watching her with a lazy smile, leaned forward to wave at her from the front row.

She returned his smile, amazed that he had driven so far, but nonetheless glad to see him. She had not liked leaving him hurt and angry. His being in the crowd seemed a good omen. Too excited to do more than barely notice the dampness at the hem of her long gown and shoes—she must have stepped in a puddle on the way in—blaming her nervousness on the odd, quivering sensation that seemed to rise from the floor itself, Elaine moved forward to introduce the Wind River Band and her first number, "Shadowed Heart."

Automatically, her hand lowered to adjust the microphone. As she reached toward the metal, a strange sensation buzzed in her fingertips causing her to instinctively draw back, startled. Again she reached for the microphone this time to take firm hold. As she did, she caught a faint crackling sound, like some ominous warning.

Before her hand could close over the steel, the floodlights suddenly extinguished, pitching the pavilion into total blackness.

* * * *

What could have happened? Had the storm somehow shorted out the power? The steady pelting of rain upon the roof and the surprised mutterings of the crowd became confused and magnified as Elaine stood immobile on the darkened stage.

Knowledge of a near-disaster caused a shaking to start in her body. She felt intense weakness, as if she had suddenly taken very ill. Blinded by the blackness, filled with a disturbing sense of disorientation, she attempted to edge from the platform back toward the side curtain. Rex hurriedly drew forward to meet her.

"Elaine, are you all right?" he asked anxiously.

"What happened?"

From somewhere behind them Oscar Macy's voice boomed above the commotion, "Now there's a lady who can really blow the lights out!"

The crowd responded with good-natured laughter. "Seriously, folks, it looks as if the storm has caused some kind of electrical problem. Just bear with us and we'll be back with the show in no time."

"It's probably nothing," Rex said, his voice still worried, "a short circuit caused by the rain."

"Did the lights just go out?"

"I knew something was wrong the minute I saw you draw back from the mike. I turned off the main switch."

Rex headed toward Levi, who kneeled with a flashlight beside wires that ran to the fuse box. Elaine remained where she was, listening to Levi's and Rex's voice muffled by Oscar's enthusiastic introduction of Denny Mack.

"Here's the problem."

Levi extended a cable to Rex. Elaine could see jagged threads of bare, exposed wire on the new, otherwise undamaged cord. It looked as if it had been jerked away with great force from the plug.

"This line was rigged to the floodlights. The bare wires were lying in a puddle of water over there, connecting with the main amplifier."

How could this be just some simple accident? Elaine drew in her breath as she thought of the power of the voltage going through that line. Rex's fast action had saved her life!

"The mike is grounded through the amp," Levi was telling her. "And the entire stage area where you were standing was damp, Elaine. It's a good thing we saw what was going on and shut off the main switch! You were a touch away from sudden death!"

Rex took the flashlight, made a few adjustments, and switched the power back on. "I was afraid to count on the fact that the fuse would have blown and stopped the current."

"That's a good thing," Levi answered abruptly, "because it wouldn't have." Levi rose, his aristocratic face grim and solemn.

"I found this inserted in place of the fuse." He held up

aluminum foil that looked like a gum wrapper.

"Someone purposefully tampered with the fuse box."

"That's jumping to conclusions," Rex said, avoiding Levi's steady gaze. "That foil could have been there for a long time. Some maintenance man could have been running some powerful equipment he knew might overload the circuit."

The exposed wire, the foil, Levi was right—the electric system had been rigged in order to commit murder!

"Shelby's to blame for this, one way or another. At the very least, he should have checked the wiring before we went on!" Levi said in condemnation.

"Go ahead! Blame me!" Shelby suddenly appeared. "I would have noticed a bare wire! I'm not stupid!"

"Carelessness is stupidity!" Levi spoke sharply. "I for one hold you totally responsible!"

"No use trying to place blame," Rex said.

"It wasn't my fault!" Shelby stalked toward the side door, but turned back, speaking in a shrill, boyish voice, "Everything was perfectly all right when I set it up!"

"What's going on?" Oscar moved quickly from the area close to the stage to join them. He watched Shelby leave before he spoke again. "What's wrong with the kid?"

Levi showed him the damaged cord and explained what had almost happened.

"Some accident!" Oscar said. "A real freak accident! But nothing bad came of it. We'll just count our blessings and go on with the show."

"No one could be that careless without meaning to,"

Levi persisted.

Oscar, to relieve the growing tension caused by Levi's remark, asked with humorous exaggeration, “Elaine, do you happen to have any enemies?”

“That's not funny,” Levi said.

Elaine was trying to sort out her thoughts. The phone call she had received before she left for the tour now echoed in her mind, ominous and threatening. With a shiver she thought about how easy it would have been in the bustle before the show for someone to have inserted the aluminum foil into the fuse box and to have severed the cord. No one would have thought it any more than an accident, the result of Shelby's carelessness or of the mixture of rain and faulty wiring within the aging structure.

Her gaze strayed toward the door Shelby had just left through. Because he had left it open, rain blew into the room, settled in low places on the worn, plank floor. Was Levi right in blaming Shelby? Could the boy have been trying to get even with Elaine for her being the cause of his not being able to play in the band tonight? Surely, adolescent grudges didn't go that far.

Levi, frowning, spoke again. “Everyone knows you always go on first, Rex.”

“In that case,” Oscar drawled, “let me rephrase my question. Rex, do *you* have any enemies?”

A loud peal of applause sounded from the hall beyond them.

“Denny must be finished,” Elaine said. “Oscar, would you announce me next? I'm going back on.”

"I'd rather you didn't," Rex interceded quickly. As if understanding how shaken she was, he insisted, "Elaine, I want you to go on back to the hotel."

Elaine answered with determination, "I promised them a song tonight. I want to go on as if nothing ever happened."

Before Rex had time to stop her, she had followed Oscar back on stage. The trauma of her near-brush with death served to push anxieties about her own performance far into the background. The crowd, unaware of the narrowly avoided disaster, cheered enthusiastically as she finished "Shadowed Heart."

Elaine suppressed a shudder of fear. The look in Rex's eyes had told her that he was keeping his true thoughts from her. No doubt Rex believed he was to have been the victim. But was that so? Hadn't someone already attempted to frighten her away from this tour?

Her eyes moved over the crowd and settled on Derrick. A single thought struck her with horror: what if Derrick, jealous of Rex and angry at her, had followed along to sabotage the tour? She quickly checked her thoughts. Derrick would never, ever harm her. But then, he wouldn't have anticipated the unscheduled change in the program. He would have expected Rex to go on first.

CHAPTER SEVEN

Elaine left her hotel room in search of Shelby. If Shelby hadn't rigged this "accident" himself, he would surely be able to supply her the names of those who had access to the electrical equipment.

She found Shelby outside the hotel, leaning against one of the pillars that braced the side porch. Elaine could tell by the way he straightened up that he was aware of her presence, yet he continued to stare sullenly out across the rain-swept darkness toward the lights of the pavilion. He looked so distraught that she began doubting the possibility that he must have been the one responsible.

"I don't want to talk to you," Shelby muttered. "Just leave me alone."

"I'm not in any way accusing you," Elaine reminded him. "I only want to find out all I can about what went on backstage tonight, and you might be able to help me."

"Aw, you're just like the rest. Blame Shelby. Why not? What has he ever done right?"

Ignoring this outburst, she asked calmly, "When did you make your last check of the equipment?"

Shelby still didn't look at her. "Right after I set it up. Like I said, the fuse was in the box, not a scrap of foil, and the wire hadn't been damaged."

"After your work was finished, did you stay backstage?"

Shelby remained silent as if cowed by the fury of the gusting wind. His wet dark hair billowed as he turned to face her. "I went to the bus for a while. Any one of them could have set this up."

Becoming more convinced that the electric shock was intended for Rex, Elaine quickly asked, "Who knew for sure that I would be going on first tonight?"

"Not me. Rex told Levi and probably Levi told the others. Why do you ask that, anyway?"

Elaine spoke candidly, "I can't see why anyone would want to harm me. They must have thought Rex would introduce the show."

The volume of the boy's voice rose. "No one would want to kill Rex. Without him, there wouldn't be any show at all."

"Control of the company..." Elaine started.

"No, you're on the wrong track," Shelby interrupted. "Besides, what makes you think it has to be one of the band members? When I returned from the bus, I found a man alone in the room. He said he'd come backstage to find you. Now that I think about it, he acted real suspicious. He hung around until Rex came in, then stomped out without a word."

Elaine's heart sank. She already knew Shelby was talking about Derrick, still she asked, "Who was he?"

"I've seen him before," Shelby said, an accusation forming in his words, "at the audition."

"Derrick Kline?"

"Yeah, that was his name, Kline. I remember. His music dragged."

"Do you know where I can find Rex?"

"He left the hotel a while ago. That might be him over at the pavilion."

The volume of the rain increased.

Shelby said above the blowing wind, "I'm not staying out here in this any longer."

She watched him duck through the back entrance of the hotel, then, determined to go on with the quest for answers, Elaine began walking toward the pavilion.

She felt lost in the whistling gale, in the pelting rain. Several times Elaine stopped and looked back through the trees, dripping wet, draped with Spanish moss that whipped in the wind. The stormy scene conjured up ghostly images that caused her to feel new stirrings of fear.

Her gaze swept through the darkness for some sign of a human form behind her. She saw no one, yet she knew how foolish it was for her to be out here alone. She should have waited for Rex to return to the hotel. She thought of heading back, but closer now to the pavilion, she, instead, increased the speed of her steps. She would be relieved to see Rex.

Levi Culver turned slowly from the fuse box he had been studying to face her. His shadowed features, the dark-tinted glasses renewed her sense of fear.

"I was looking for Rex."

"He's back at the hotel."

Elaine, shivering from her drenched clothing, spoke again. "Is there any way what happened tonight could have been just a simple accident?"

"In this back-woods place," Levi replied, "anything is possible. The wiring is out-dated. And, of course, the cord could have been damaged in transport."

"But you don't think so."

He took off his glasses. Steady, gray eyes held to hers. This gesture seemed to transform him, made him appear too straight-forward, too honest, to conceal his real thoughts. "No."

"Shelby told me my friend, Derrick Kline, was back stage before the show started. Did you happen to notice him?"

"Yes," Levi replied. "He hung around a while waiting for you. But he wasn't the only one back here. I saw Denny Mack near the equipment. But, then, Denny always gives Shelby a hand. Rex had assigned this job to Shelby."

An implication was evident in his words.

"Surely Shelby wouldn't hate Rex enough to purposefully tamper with the equipment."

"Rex didn't say so, but I know that he thinks Shelby set this up to disrupt the show. Even if I could prove Shelby had done this, I would never be able to convince Rex that it wasn't just an impulsive, childish act. He would think that Shelby wasn't even aware of the possible consequences."

"That would be hard to believe."

Levi's unwavering gaze unsettled her. "If you ask me, Rex made a great mistake taking Shelby on this tour."

A sudden, clattering noise caused them both to start, but it was only the wind dislodging a piece of wood above the frame of the open door.

"Next this old relic will blow over," he said cynically, then he returned to the subject at hand. "Some people just aren't salvageable."

"The boy could just be going through one of those rebellious stages," Elaine remarked.

"If not for Rex, he would be going to reform school."

"Did Shelby," Elaine ventured, "know Rex was not going on first tonight?"

"Rex told me about his change of plans, of course. I had to tell Oscar and Denny, but anyone might have overheard."

"Who else might want to harm Rex or the show?"

Levi's next words, so openly truthful, startled her. "On the surface it looks as if everything's fine between the tour members. But when you stop to examine motives, there's plenty. When Bill Craft selected Rex as his business partner, he made him a very wealthy, much-envied man."

"If something had happened to Rex tonight," Elaine asked, "how would it affect the company?"

"CMP would revert fully to Lisa Craft. But Lisa couldn't run it. She would waste no time getting someone to take Rex's place."

"Who would that be?"

"One of us. Probably Oscar…or me."

"Denny Mack wouldn't be considered?"

"Denny was never in line for a management job. But there's no end to the hard feelings between Rex and him. As you've probably noticed, Denny's got a bad case of the "big star" complex."

"Professional jealousy," Elaine said. "But that's hardly reason enough for murder."

The word *murder* caused a chill to go through Elaine. Levi, as if he had not ruled out the act as an attempted murder, didn't object.

"Much as they dislike each other, Denny wouldn't reap any particular benefit from Rex's death," Levi said. "The only ones who would gain financially are Lisa and Shelby. Rex has provided for Shelby generously in his will, and the boy knows it. As his heir, Shelby would stand to inherit Rex's mansion in New Orleans, property in Wyoming, and a small fortune in stocks and cash."

Elaine looked back at the ancient, gray box that contained the row after row of old fuses. "I can be grateful to Rex for pulling that switch in time."

"I think Rex and I noticed the problem at the same instant."

It had struck Elaine as highly unusual that Rex would let an amateur like herself introduce the show. For a moment the fact became sinister. With Levi standing beside him, Rex knew that if he didn't cut off the power, Levi would. That left Rex with no choice. He had been forced into taking the action that saved her life.

* * * *

The very moment she returned to her room, Derrick called and asked her to meet him for dinner in an hour. Elaine slipped into dry clothes, but not anxious to see him, remained in her room. She stood by the window where wind and rain battered against the fragile glass. She watched the black, swaying branches of the cypress trees.

A heavy weight had settled over her heart. The idea that Rex had set this all up himself in order to eliminate her made no sense at all, yet it remained an ugly shadow, in the back of her mind.

Wearily she turned around, just as a tap sounded on the door.

"Who's there?"

A soft voice answered, "Lisa Craft." She added as she slipped into Elaine's room, "Remember me?"

Who could forget the lovely Lisa Craft, famous singer, part owner of Craft Productions, Rex's partner? The fashionable, black dress Lisa wore added just the right touch of mystery and dignity to her appearance.

"I had no idea you were here."

"I wouldn't miss your first performance." Lisa replied, smiling graciously. "It really amazed me. Rex was right. You do have a special talent."

Lisa crossed the room, pausing to look from the window before she turned and silently regarded Elaine.

"I wouldn't tell Rex this for fear he would cancel the show," she said at last, "but I'm really worried over what happened tonight."

"Frankly, so am I."

Elaine felt the presence of a barrier between them. It might be caused by Lisa's air, much too practiced, much too polished. Lisa stepped forward.

"I'm going to be entirely honest with you, Elaine, because I believe in being fair."

Elaine waited for her to go on.

"A short time ago, I began getting threatening phone calls. I tried to have them traced. Each time a voice warned me not to be part of this tour."

Surprised, Elaine said, "I received a call exactly like that just before I left New Orleans."

"We meet all sorts of kooks in this business. At first I thought some crazy fan had a thing for me. But after tonight, I'm beginning to have second thoughts."

"What do you think is behind these calls?"

"We're a big company, we make lots of enemies. Maybe some rejected singer or writer has got it in for, not just me, but for the entire show."

Elaine studied her. She usually had no trouble detecting falseness. Lisa's stagy manner convinced Elaine that Lisa was accustomed to dealing in partial truths or even in outright lies. She could resent Elaine's role in the show, the one she had impulsively given up. Possibly Lisa herself had put someone up to making that phone call to Elaine. It could be part of some scheme Lisa had hatched up to scare Elaine and keep her from completing the tour. But what would be her reason? Jealousy over Rex?

As if Lisa could read Elaine's thoughts, she said, "I'm not as brave as you are, Elaine. Those calls frightened me.

That's why I quit the tour. I thought it was me he was after. But the calls stopped once I left the show."

Lisa fell silent, violet eyes large and dark.

"This is not just some sick person's idea of a joke. As you can see, it's gone beyond that. Whoever this weirdo is, he's transferred his interest from me to you, as my replacement. Anyway, I thought you had the right to know."

Lisa crossed back to the door. Keeping one hand on the knob, she turned back. "If you want a release from your contract, I'll talk to Rex."

Was Lisa trying to warn Elaine or trying to frighten her away?

Elaine replied quickly, "No, I intend to finish the tour."

CHAPTER EIGHT

Derrick had chosen the best table in the dining room, one beside the rustic fireplace with its pleasant, crackling fire. He gave a slow, easy smile as he watched Elaine approach.

"You and me," he said, "just like old times."

The suspicion about him that had been building up in her mind immediately vanished. Derrick, her old friend, had driven so far to attend tonight's performance and show his support.

Elaine seated herself across from him and for a moment the terrifying experience at the pavilion began to take distance. She started to feel at ease, comfortable, just as she did at their safe little table at The Highlands.

"All we need is Thad," she said, returning his smile.

"Wanted him to drive out here with me," Derrick replied, "but you know Thad. Too busy cutting his big deals."

As he spoke, he lifted a menu. "Let's see if they can cook a steak as good as Thad's."

Before Elaine could answer she spotted Rex standing in

the doorway, his eyes opaque and serious as they met hers. She felt her breath catch as he strode directly toward them.

Rex now wore a white shirt, slightly open at the throat. Locks of black hair, curled from the moisture, spilled across his forehead. "Why don't you two join me for dinner?" he suggested.

Derrick did not even glance up from the menu, but said curtly, "We like it right here."

"But you can join us," Elaine cut in quickly, anxious to take the edge off Derrick's rudeness.

"Some of the others will show up," Rex replied. "I'll just get another table." He hesitated a moment, eyes dark and unreadable, holding to hers. "I'll talk to you later, Elaine."

Derrick took charge of the ordering. As he talked to the waitress, Elaine's gaze wandered toward Rex. He sat alone at a table near the porch. He did not look at her, but gazed at the window as if he were able to see through the drawn drapes into the darkness outside.

Disquiet filled her. Elaine longed to be over there with Rex. But that was not possible, not after she had accepted Derrick's invitation for dinner.

"Would you believe it?" Derrick was saying, astonished.. "Lisa Craft is here."

Elaine turned just as Lisa, chic and poised in her black dress, made a grand entrance. She stopped at their table, glancing from Derrick to Lisa.

"I just loved that song you sang tonight, 'Shadowed Heart,'" she said.

Elaine could detect no trace of hostility in Lisa's voice, no hint of regret that she had not been the one singing onstage. In fact, the compliment sounded warm and sincere.

"Thank you. Lisa, have you met Derrick Kline? He's a singer, too."

"We've met," Lisa said, casting an admiring glance toward Derrick. "It's my business to know all the good singers."

"I tried out for this show," Derrick responded.

Lisa waved away his evident disappointment and said, "For this tour, we really needed a female. But that doesn't mean you can't audition for us again."

Derrick brightened. "I sing regularly at The Highlands," he boasted, eager to impress Lisa.

"Call me, then," Lisa said hurriedly as she moved on toward Rex's table.

Rex rose. Elaine thought of the many photos she had seen of the two of them, standing close together, smiling. Recalling those perfect images in the tabloids made her glance away.

Derrick remained staring directly at them, his lean features furrowed with a sharp frown. Elaine knew Derrick was given to dark periods of jealous brooding, and she was aware that this emotion had surfaced in him now. Rex was talking to Lisa, but his gaze had strayed to Elaine. As always, Elaine, captured by his blue-black eyes, felt unable to look back at Derrick.

"Mr. Big Shot," Derrick said under his breath. Then he

tried to restore himself, reaching for Elaine's hand, and saying worriedly, "I'm really puzzled about that deal with the wiring."

Elaine forced her attention back to Derrick. "Let's not talk about that now," she suggested. "Let's just enjoy our meal."

...As if that were going to be possible, with the beautiful Lisa Craft seated across from Rex. She didn't look toward their table, yet she was aware of Rex, the way Rex's glance flitted to Derrick's hand that covered hers, the way his smile slowly vanished.

"I like that Oscar Macy," Derrick was saying with a gusto he wasn't feeling. "Macy and you really kept the show going. Saved it from being a real disaster."

After the long, awkward dinner ended, Derrick and she left the dining area, left Lisa and Rex lingering over coffee. They parted in the lobby. Feeling restless, unable to sleep, Elaine did not go up to her room. Maybe in the back of her mind she was harboring the thought that she would be able to talk to Rex tonight.

She wandered outside and remained for a while in front of the lodge. Tonight's storm had at last blown over, and wanting a breath of fresh air, she ambled toward the lounge area to the side of the hotel.

There she could remain in the dimness of the porch and view the night, now quiet and peaceful. She entered the huge, screened-in annex that opened into the dining area. She sank down on one of the worn chairs and tried to blot out all of her thoughts and fears.

Soon she became aware of voices through the thin wall that separated her from the dining room. Lisa Craft was speaking.

"You know I wasn't serious about quitting the tour, Rex."

"But you did quit," Rex responded tersely.

"I didn't expect you to replace me quite so soon."

Elaine felt a tightening around her heart. She was hearing the truth Lisa had not spoken to her. She now knew just why Lisa had shown up here tonight. A fight with Rex, a lover's quarrel, had been behind her impulsive decision to abandon the tour. Lisa intended to patch things up with Rex and take back her staring role. Elaine could visualize the two of them still seated at the table, Lisa so lovely in her black dress.

"I want us to be together again, Rex. I can't believe you would rather be singing with her than with me."

"You just don't have any capacity for being faithful, do you?" Rex, his voice, low and sardonic, continued, "Whoever you were seeing while we were dating, you're still seeing. I've believed your lies before, but not this time. It's over between us. We're business partners, nothing more."

"All right, then," Lisa said coldly, "let's talk business. You know the state of the company's finances as well as I do. We're losing more money than we're making."

"And whose fault is that? You refuse to listen to Levi or to me. You plunge in without even consulting us. Then you hand over your bad decisions for us to fix."

Ignoring him, Lisa continued. “We're going to have to come up with some gigantic boost if we're going to survive.”

Elaine, feeling guilty for eavesdropping, started to leave, but strains of music, familiar strains, drew her back. Startled, Elaine recognized her father's voice, rich and clear, singing, “Silver Bayou dreamer, Hide away from life, Live alone in shadows...”

Elaine listened aghast. What was Lisa doing with her father's song? The tape clicked off, and Lisa said, again coldly, “I'm about to nail down the biggest deal of my career. Not that I expect any co-operation from you. You never agree with me on anything. If you don't want to record the album, Denny will.”

“Why do you think I've been buying up all the rights to his work? Of course I want to record this album! But the last time I talked to Thad, he said Elaine didn't want to sell that particular song, or any of his unpublished collection.”

Elaine felt choked by Rex's betrayal. Rex had known she was S.S. Sands daughter, that's why he had hired her in the first place. Rex wanted to be the first to sing and record “Silver Bayou Dreamer,” the very work he had refused to let her introduce on the tour, the one she had believed he hadn't even liked!

Another bitter betrayal gripped her. The only copy of her father's last songs was in her private filing cabinet above her cousin's club. Could Thad be involved? Elaine remembered the many times Thad had tried to get her to turn over to him the “Louisiana Drifter” songs, his anxiousness for her to agree to let him sell them, his impatience at her refusal. There could be only one explanation. Thad had taken the songs and offered them to CMP without her permission! But Thad, her direct heir, her only living relative, could not sell them without her signature. The idea of what Thad had done filled her with hurt and anger, then with chilling suspicion.

CHAPTER NINE

After hours of ringing the club, Elaine finally got through to Thad. "How's big-time?" he asked happily. "I'm so glad you called. We have business to discuss."

Elaine felt relieved. She wasn't going to have to ask him about his negotiations with Craft Music Productions. He intended to tell her outright.

To her surprise, instead of talking about CMP, Thad began to discuss Derrick.

"Rumors are beginning to circulate around The Highlands."

"What rumors?" Elaine asked.

He hesitated, as if he were being forced to tell her something she should know.

"About Derrick and some woman he's been seeing, some singer. I'm going to find out all the details for you."

Elaine certainly hadn't expected this. She quickly replied, "You don't need to. Derrick and I have never been anything more than friends."

"Some friend!" Thad snorted.

Many years her senior, Thad had always looked after

her interests—at least that was what she had always believed.

"You know what I'm thinking? You should break off with Derrick completely."

"We have nothing to break off," Elaine said insistently.

"Look at you, Elaine. S.S. Sands' daughter, touring with Rex Tobin! I predict your career is going to skyrocket."

Thad's enthusiastic words drew to a sudden halt, icing over as he added, "Now's the time to buy Derrick out, before you cut a gold or platinum record."

Always the agent, Thad hurried to explain.

"Strapped as Derrick is for money, he'll be happy to sign away for a few bucks all the rights to the songs you two wrote together. Then you won't have to worry about splitting any future royalties with him."

"But that would be almost like cheating him."

"You wrote most of the lyrics anyway. Derrick's spent years sponging off your talent. You should faze him out, now, while you can cut a cheap deal!"

"That's what it would be," Elaine remarked, "a cheap deal. I'm not interested. But I didn't call you tonight to discuss Derrick. I want to know all about the offer you made to Lisa Craft."

During the silence that fell on the other end of the line, Elaine thought about how badly Thad, his reasons unknown to her at the time, had wanted her to audition for this tour. A picture of The Highlands came to her, the shabbiness of the faded stage curtains, the few late-hour customers still listening to music. She visualized Thad's craggy face and knew that the lines about his eyes had deepened.

"I can explain everything, Elaine."

She could hear his intake of breath, which now sounded very weary.

"Just after the news of your father's death hit the papers, Lisa Craft contacted me. She said CMP was already in the process of buying the exclusive rights to all of your father's recorded songs. But they were especially seeking out new material, anything he might have written that hadn't already been sold. She told me they planned to compile an album of his best work."

Elaine made no reply.

"Of course, I knew all about the "Louisiana Drifter" collection. Your father had promised to turn the songs over to me as agent before he died. Since he never gave them to me, I knew you had copies of them."

"Why did you keep this a secret from me?"

"You had just lost your father. You told me right out that you had no intention of selling his last work. I also knew I had to act fast, before the company lost interest. So I took copies of "Silver Bayou Dreamer" and all his other unpublished songs from your files and brought them down to CMP, just to see what they were willing to offer."

"You mean you took Dad's work without even asking me?"

Thad ignored her question.

"Rex loved the songs. He tried to close right then and there, but I point-blank told him that you were unwilling to sell. Besides that, I said, Lisa and I were having trouble agreeing on a contract. You don't realize just how much cash they're willing to lay on the line. I know I shouldn't have, but I didn't want to tell you until I had the whole package cinched. Then I felt you couldn't possibly say no."

"How much money are they offering?"

"A fifty-thousand dollar advance for exclusive rights plus a cut of the sales! Just think what kind of money we're talking about! And what a tribute it would be to Uncle Steven to have a man like Rex Tobin sing his songs, a singer who has consistently made hit records, gold ones!"

"Rex didn't mention any of this to me."

"That's because I made Rex promise not to. I let him know exactly how you felt, and how it might be impossible to talk you into selling the songs despite the size of the offer."

Thad's manner became lighter.

"But what an offer, Elaine! Thanks to my charm, Lisa has at last agreed to all my terms." Thad chuckled. "You see, I asked for a more sizable percent of the royalties than they are accustomed to giving. I've always known Uncle Steven was going to be a legend someday, and I am determined that you're going to reap the profit from it! But, Elaine, this is important to me, too. I do need the commission in the worst way. You are going to sign the papers, aren't you?"

"No, Thad, I'm not. I may decide to sell the collection some day, but certainly not now."

"Elaine, you can't be serious! We'll never get another

chance like this!"

"Then we won't. I'm sorry, Thad, but this is the only decision I can make right now."

Elaine detected great bitterness in his voice.

"The songs belong to you, not me," he said, "but you're making a big mistake."

* * * *

Unable to sleep, Elaine wandered back down into the lobby. She found Derrick seated near the stone fireplace.

"I thought you had left for New Orleans," she said.

"I wanted to talk to you again. I've been trying to ring your room," he said, "but your line's always tied up."

He rose, lank brown hair spilling across his forehead.

"Elaine, I'm sorry about the way I've been acting. That's why I drove up here tonight, to apologize."

He moved closer, taking both her hands in his.

"I was so worried when the lights went out when you were on stage. I've been talking to Levi and some of the others." A dark scowl appeared on Derrick's face. "I think it was more than just some minor trouble with the wiring."

"The storm..." Elaine began.

Derrick interrupted, "It had nothing to do with the storm." His voice raised, a loud, ringing warning in the deserted lobby. "Elaine, I'm going to tell you straight out, I don't like your being on this show."

His hands gripped hers tighter.

"In fact, honey, I want you go back with me to New Orleans tonight."

"Derrick, you know that's just not possible. I've signed

with the tour. I can't just quit."

Derrick's thin lips became tight as if he were suppressing some great resentment. "That's not the real reason, is it? You want to stay because of Rex Tobin! But let me tell you something, Rex Tobin is all for himself. If you hang around him, you'll only end up getting hurt."

Derrick's voice softened a little.

"If I were touring with you, then I could look after you. But I just don't want you to go on alone, not without me."

The pace of his words slowed, transformed into the lazy drawl so familiar to her.

"In fact, Elaine, I want you to come home and marry me."

Marry Derrick? Elaine had never even considered the idea. And Derrick had never even so much as hinted about having special feelings for her. If, indeed, he did. Elaine regarded him with surprise, hoping to see some teasing light in his large, hazel eyes. Derrick looked, she thought with sinking heart, totally earnest.

"But you're seeing someone else," Elaine said. "What about her? Who is she, Derrick?"

He avoided her question, saying, "You're the one I care about."

"You know we've never discussed marriage. We haven't actually even dated. I'm not in love with you and I don't believe you're in love with me."

"You can't say that, Elaine. It's just not true."

A frown cut across Derrick's lean face, making him look immensely angry.

BITTER MELODY

Jackson / Britton

"You must know I feel about you! Don't think for a minute I'm going to let Rex Tobin steal you away from me!"

CHAPTER TEN

Early the next morning Elaine spotted Levi waiting impatiently outside the hotel's gift shop. Even idle, he looked totally businesslike, a little pressed for time. Even though she eased slowly into a discussion of Lisa Craft, Elaine's question caught him completely off-guard. "Do you know who Lisa is dating now?"

For the first time since she had met him, Levi did not have a ready response. He faltered before he replied.

"She was seeing Rex, but I hear she's found herself another singer. No one knows just who he is, but we will soon, you can count on that. Lisa will want to promote him through the company."

Elaine thought about the stark, hostile look on Derrick's face last night as he had stared toward the table where Lisa had been seated with Rex. Lisa, not she, might have been the cause of Derrick's jealousy.

Levi glanced impatiently into the gift shop.

"Let's go on in and see if we can speed up the shopping."

Denny Mack stood just inside the door watching Rex as

he tried on a black Stetson trimmed with sterling silver. Rex examined the workmanship.

"I've never seen a design quite like this one."

Blue eyes smiled as they met Elaine's.

"What do you think?"

"Just buy it," Levi answered, consulting his watch.

"Always has to have the best, doesn't he?" Denny Mack muttered.

"Why do you care?" Levi shot back acidly. "You will end up with a hat just like it."

Levi turned to show Elaine the watch he wore, one exquisitely inlaid with turquoise. With a grin the red-bearded Denny immediately pushed up his own sleeve revealing an identical watch.

"Trying to get the best of everyone else, Mr. Mack," Levi said, "is going to be your downfall."

Still smiling, the undaunted Denny asked, "So, what shall we buy today, Levi?"

Elaine watched as Rex began paying for his purchase. After over-hearing his conversation with Lisa, Elaine could not bring herself to wait for him, but made a hurried exit.

* * * *

"Maybe what happened last night wasn't an accident after all," Oscar Macy announced as he boarded the bus. "What we could be dealing with here is the antithesis of a fan club."

Oscar's joking words fell upon dreary silence.

"It's obvious the membership plans to exterminate us one by one," Oscar's pale blue eyes squinted from one tour member to another. "Let's draw straws to see who goes on first tonight."

"Are we going to have to listen to this all the way to Houston?" Shelby moaned.

"Where's Rex?" Levi said, looking up from his notebook. "It's time we get started."

"Partied too late last night," Oscar replied. "If I weren't such a family man, I'd have done the same thing." He glanced toward Elaine. "Everyone's single but me, you know. After three years Levi has at last finalized his divorce. And Denny and Shelby, here, are just kids. Don't even know about the girls yet."

Denny, who took great pains to look younger than his forty-some years, immediately bristled.

"Compared to you, old man, everyone's a kid!"

Elaine's gaze shifted from Denny to Levi, who was writing figures into a ledger. Since overhearing the secret plot to record her father's songs, Elaine had believed that she, indeed, might have been the killer's target, but as she watched Levi write number after number, she realized that Rex was really the one in danger. High stakes were involved, like the take-over of Craft Music Productions.

In the stillness she listened to the clank-clank of the heavy weights Denny was lifting. Oscar strolled past him to the wall mirror. He stood smoothing his thick, graying hair. "I think I'll change my image," he announced in a loud, theatrical voice. "Maybe dip my hair in a bucket of dye."

Elaine wished he would not tease Denny. Everyone knew Denny was sensitive about his age, that he took great pains to keep the gray from overtaking his reddish hair and beard.

"Then I could be a big star, just like Denny Mack!"

Elaine could not help smiling at Oscar's primping motions. Soon he strutted away, sucking in his big stomach, flexing his muscles. "My tag, *Big Oscar Macy*, isn't getting me anywhere. I think I'll change my name. What do you think, Elaine? How about *Macho Macy*?"

"How about *Granddaddy Corn Pone*?" Denny snapped.

Instead of taking offense, Oscar laughed. Elaine didn't approve of Oscar's deviling Denny, but she did like his appreciative laughter when the joke reversed.

Denny set down the weights.

All trace of teasing drained from his voice as he said to Elaine, "When Rex tried so hard to get Macy back on the show, I told him not to bother. What we don't need are has-beens!"

Denny Mack's vanity, often expressed in envy, did not set well with Elaine. She immediately sprung to Oscar's defense. "Without Oscar the show would have no life! Everyone loves him!"

Oscar smiled at her. Elaine felt at that moment they had formed a solid friendship.

* * * *

The moment Rex entered, Denny Mack, still mad at Oscar, laid down his weights and said, "I want to drive."

"Fine."

Rex was addressing Denny, but he was gazing at Elaine. She looked away, taking the seat at the table near the window. To her disconcertion Rex headed directly toward her. He removed his black Stetson, placed it on the table, and took the chair across from her. She did not meet his gaze, but she was aware of his handsome, slightly rugged features, his crisp, black hair, ruffled from the hat. She stared down at the Stetson, at the ornate, silver hatband, with its strange, geometric design, then quickly drew out her notebook.

"Working on one of your songs?" he asked.

"That's what I do when I have a spare moment," she answered, unable to keep the coldness from her voice.

The notes, in a neat line, had remained unchanged since she had first jotted them down at The Highlands, but she was not satisfied with the words. As the bus rolled along the highway, she, not glancing toward Rex, added and scratched out lines. No matter how hard she tried, she could not find the right words for the ending.

"May I see what you're working on?"

She reluctantly slid the papers toward him.

Rex sang in a low tone, "Or did we fall in love with, the glitter of the road?"

He gazed toward her, smoky blue eyes radiating approval. Was his admiration for her song or for her? Or was this only a show, part of some highly-skilled falseness, another one of his deceits? Still, the bitterness of her questions did not prevent Elaine from feeling breathless, just as she had the first time their eyes had met.

Rex took a pen from his shirt pocket, made a correction in the music and scribbled a notation in reference to the chords in the margin. Then he sang the line again.

"Yes, that is exactly what it needed. Now it is perfect!"

"Except it doesn't have a final line."

Oscar, who had been tuning his guitar, suddenly broke in, "Hand it over to me."

Rex obliged, and with Oscar's music, Elaine's song sprang expertly to life. "I haven't heard such a good tune," he said, once he had finished playing, "since the one you wanted to sing at the audition, 'Silver Bayou Dreamer'. That little song just keeps running through my mind."

Elaine's gaze strayed to Rex, surprised by the way Oscar's words had altered him. He had become strangely distant, his eyes, dark and remote.

Rex's helpful assistance, his smiles, had almost swayed her. She had almost been convinced that Rex would never do anything underhand. As she studied him now, she thought only of his conversation with Lisa and the double-dealing between Thad and Craft Music Productions. Oscar interrupted her accusing thoughts.

"I've got your last line!" His booming voice, tinged with humorous, exaggerated sadness, sang, "Don't you think I should have know'd, that someday you would leave me, for the glitter of the road!"

Rex's quick smile revealed a flash of strong, white teeth.

"I'm afraid that won't do. People like happy endings. Not to mention good grammar." Then he added seriously, "What we need is a positive line."

He turned toward Elaine.

"How about, 'And we will have each other, And the glitter of the road.'"

"Will you make a copy for me?" Oscar asked eagerly. "The boys and I need something new and first-rate to use for practice."

Trying not to share Oscar's enthusiasm, Elaine did as he requested, then in the same wooden way, closed her notebook.

"Thank you, Rex. My song is finished. At last."

Elaine did not feel elated over the perfect lines Rex had supplied. She tried, in fact, not to think of him or of the show scheduled in Houston tonight. She gazed from the window where steamy mist drifted up from pools of rain. The flat land had some time ago become gently rolling hills. The trees had changed, too, no longer sweeping with Spanish moss, but tall, rugged, unadorned.

"Anyone for poker?" Oscar's voice sounded above the hum of the motor.

"Sure," Shelby said, scampering from the couch where he had been dozing.

"No matter how many times you get beat, you keep coming back for more, don't you?" Oscar drawled.

"So do I." Rex admitted as he joined them at the table.

"You said you could play, Elaine," Oscar invited.

"She's not going to play!" Shelby moaned. "We'll have to stop every few minutes and explain the rules to her."

His derogatory tone caused Elaine to rise to the challenge.

Elaine regarded the cards Oscar dealt her. Automatically she shifted the two queens and pair of deuces to one side just as Thad would have done. She asked for another card, then slid forward two coins. "I'll open."

Rex silently met her bid. Oscar shook his head.

"Good thing you folded."

Shelby abruptly slid quarters into the center. "No one can beat this hand."

"I think you're bluffing," Elaine said. "I'll raise three."

Rex laid down his hand.

"Too rich for me."

Shelby pushed his last coins into the pot.

Elaine met Shelby's raise and called.

"Two aces and two kings!" Shelby cried out triumphantly.

Elaine lowered her cards.

"Two deuces and three queens. Full house."

Shelby's eye widened. He stared toward her with new-found respect.

"Just because I don't look like a poker player," Elaine said, "you immediately jumped to conclusions."

She paused, turning away from Shelby, speaking directly to Rex. "People aren't always what they appear to be."

CHAPTER ELEVEN

Wanting to avoid Rex, Elaine did not join the others in the hotel dining room, but slipped across the street to a small cafe. Before she had finished eating, Shelby, whom she hadn't noticed standing at the counter, moved to her table, tray heaped with hamburger and fries. He didn't ask if he could join her, just slipped into the booth and without even a hello began eating.

Elaine took his presence as a kind of acceptance, an effort on his part to put hard feelings behind them. Elaine searched for something to say.

"Have you ever played in Houston before?" she asked eventually.

"Rex always schedules Houston," Shelby replied.

The sudden jerk of his head called attention to his shoulder-length, dark hair and the half-hidden, silver earring.

"According to Rex, tonight's all important. We either succeed here or the tour's a flop."

"Do you sing?"

"Not good enough for Rex Tobin. Soon I'm going to

form my own band! Maybe Denny and I will start up together. He's got a real sense of beat. You might have noticed, neither of us fit into this hick-music scene."

"I would hardly call it that." Elaine smiled. "This type of music belongs to America. It's very popular."

"Your songs drag," Shelby said condemningly. "But I could give them that special touch they need."

"I've worked hard to achieve a certain effect. I'm not interested in changing my style."

"You ought to be thinking of your future. If you're ever going to make it big, you'll have to break off, maybe with Denny and me. Rex is never going to put the spotlight on anyone but himself! If Denny or you or I want to get noticed, we'll have to do it on our own. That's why he doesn't want me playing while you sing."

"That's not the reason, Shelby. Rex knows that my songs weren't meant for a fast drum beat."

Shelby studied her, a dark scowl appearing on his face.

"You're just like Lisa Craft, aren't you? Scared to cross him!"

"Lisa doesn't seem the least bit intimidated by Rex, or anyone else."

"Lisa puts up a good front. The truth is she's afraid of Rex. Everyone knows that's why she quit the tour."

Shelby's words caused a tightness in Elaine's throat. She hadn't considered the possibility that last night Lisa had been warning her about Rex.

"Rex never wanted her as a partner in the first place. In fact, Rex has been doing his best to oust her so he can get one of his puppets, probably Levi Culver, and take complete control of CMP himself. That's what he wants, control. See how he tries to control Denny and me."

"If he wants a puppet, he shouldn't be thinking of Levi. He's a take-charge sort of man himself."

Shelby laughed.

"Just another act! Culver's own company went belly-up because he's a bungler. But Rex couldn't wait to talk him into joining Craft's. Losers are all Rex wants around him."

"You sound very ungrateful."

The thought crossed Elaine's mind that Shelby did not really believe half of what he was saying, but was simply echoing what Denny Mack had told him. Why was Denny trying so hard to turn Shelby against Rex?

"If I disliked someone as much as you do Rex, I certainly wouldn't be working for him."

Shelby shrugged.

"It's either that or go to Riemyers."

Riemyers must be a reform school or a group home for delinquent youths. Elaine's vexation increased. Shelby was just a self-centered adolescent, too immature to realize that Rex was probably the only real friend he had.

"Rex is giving you the chance of a lifetime. You should appreciate the opportunity to learn from him and work with him."

"No one can work with him," Shelby countered. "You should have heard the fight he had with Lisa right before this tour!"

Lisa's talk of her warning phone calls sprang to Elaine's

mind. Had the threats been directed only at Lisa? Had the call Elaine received been only a ploy to redirect suspicion.

"Rex isn't the man you think he is!"

The pressure of Shelby's warning caused Elaine to consider another possibility. No one was intended to be harmed by the rigged electricity. It, too, was part of a ruse and would be used later when Lisa was found murdered. Fingers of fear gripped Elaine. She must not allow Shelby's reckless words to sway her. She lifted her cup and took another drink of strong coffee.

"Rex used to be different," Shelby confessed reluctantly. "We used to be friends. Only now, he's on my case all the time. I can't do anything to please him."

"Maybe you're not giving Rex a chance."

"He's not giving *me* a chance! See how he blamed me about the wiring. I swear, Elaine, it wasn't my fault!"

Elaine had to be very careful now not to estrange Shelby when he seemed, for the first time, willing to confide in her. She noted the boy's earnest expression, and sensed that he was telling the truth.

"I believe you."

"I want to go on tonight," Shelby pleaded, dark eyes entreating, as if it were the only thing in the world that mattered to him. "Will you put in a good word for me?"

For a long moment, Elaine regarded Shelby.

"I'll try," she said finally. "But only if you promise to follow instructions."

"It's a deal!"

* * * *

That night, Elaine slipped into the silver-blue dress Thad had helped her select and paused to view the effect. Rex considered this show the most important one on the tour. Every detail concerning tonight must be perfect.

She kept thinking of her last appearance and the disaster so narrowly averted. If someone were trying to sabotage Rex Tobin's show, would he strike again tonight?

Rex, in the lobby, watched her approach. He wore a deep blue suit, carefully tailored to fit his broad shoulders and trim waist, an outfit that harmonized perfectly with the color of her dress. Rex's eyes lit as they locked on hers. He stood very straight for a moment, then stepped forward.

"You couldn't be more beautiful," he said tenderly.

Elaine did not allow herself to fall under his spell, even though he sounded sincere.

"I looked for you in the dining room," he continued.

"I wasn't hungry."

Outside, dark clouds had gathered. The building where they were to perform was so close they did not take the bus. They crossed the busy intersection together, Levi and Oscar bringing up the rear. At the first sight of the tremendous auditorium, Elaine felt a strange foreboding, as if tonight would be the scene of another disaster.

The tiring bus ride, then settling into the hotel without a minute to rest, had left her physically shaken. That, on top of an entire night without sleep, made her doubt that she could perform her part of the show with any skill.

"Shelby wants to play so much tonight," she told Rex, remembering her promise to put in a good word for the boy.

"It's up to you, Elaine. Do you actually want him on stage when you are?"

"I think he's learned his lesson."

They entered the huge hall through side doors that led backstage. The equipment had already been set up and Rex began immediately to re-check everything.

When Shelby came in, Rex said, "You're back on. But you'd better understand I don't want any of your foolishness. We've got too much at stake!"

Rex turned to Elaine, "I've changed the schedule. You're not to go on first. I've decided to open."

Oscar's hand slid to his side as if drawing a make-believe gun from a holster.

"I'll keep you covered," he drawled.

Laughter eased the tension.

"The rest of the show will follow as scheduled. I'll end the performance, as usual." He turned to Levi, saying in a serious voice, "I don't want anyone backstage but our group."

Elaine remained in her dressing room for a while, then came out to stand at the corner of the velvet curtain where she could see the immense auditorium with its three balconies. She watched with apprehension as the audience began to arrive. Oscar drew forward to stand beside her. Together they continued to watch the ever-growing crowd.

"Do you suppose they really know good music from bad?" he asked with a chuckle.

"Yes, they do," Rex said from behind them. "And you,

Oscar, of all people, know it."

Would the crowd ever stop pouring into the hall? At last every row, even in the upper levels, seemed packed to capacity. Elaine skimmed faces hopefully, wishing she could spot either Derrick or Thad.

The opening occurred with rapid pace. The crimson curtain parted and the spotlight fell upon Rex. He at once became the perfect master of ceremonies, his every gesture and expression smooth and practiced. After his introduction, he sang a simple love song. Elaine had never heard anyone express so beautifully such powerful emotion.

Elaine, like the audience, was held captive. In the dreamy haze of the moment she felt as she had at The Highlands, as if Rex were singing to her alone. At length she was brought back to reality by the thunderous sound of applause. Rex remained on stage and Levi and he sang a number highlighted by the perfect timing and smoothness achieved by many years of association.

Rex stepped back to play the guitar and Levi sang two songs by himself. His act had polish, perfection Elaine couldn't help but admire. The show was progressing beautifully. All she had to do is make certain her part of it kept up the standard.

Denny Mack changed the pace, his tenor voice high and rich above a background of drums, brass and piano. Elaine would follow Oscar, a hard act to follow. His wonderful music was interspaced with jokes that left the crowd roaring with laughter. He began playing a lively song while the crowd clapped and sang along. As he strummed the banjo faster and faster, Elaine almost forgot that she would be onstage next and that this was going to be the first time she had sang alone to such a vast audience.

Dryness parched her throat. Of all times for bad memories to surface, her girlhood failure, the singing of "Danny Boy" at The Highlands, arose like a ghost to haunt her. Rex Tobin stepped to the microphone, his hand out-stretched toward her.

"We've added a new member to the Wind River Boys," It's my privilege to introduce—Elaine Sands!"

Elaine walked onstage, greeted by loud cheers and whistling. Smiling, Rex leaned closer to the microphone again.

"They don't seem to think of you as one of the boys, Elaine."

Laughter followed, then Rex, his guitar in hand, stepped away, leaving Elaine alone in the spotlighted area. Whoever had rigged last night's disaster, was he watching her now? Had he been watching, waiting though all the numbers for her to step on stage? Was he going to strike at any time?

She introduced her song, successful at keeping the terrible anxiety she felt from sounding in her voice. She scanned the great mass of watchers. She must do as Rex had advised, free herself from all the dark memories, from everything but her message. Elaine reached out for the microphone, half expecting it to hiss and spark and for the hall to fall into blackness.

"I would like to sing one of my latest songs, 'You

Didn't Love Me Yesterday.'"

She had selected this song to open because it meant more to her than the others. She could feel the emotion of the words and felt sure she could sing them with ease and accuracy. Elaine gazed out across the sea of faces. The beginning lines opened well, then to Elaine's horror Shelby crossed over to the drums. Just as in the audition, the sudden, fast drumbeat made her lose her sense of timing. Her voice faltered.

Their success at Houston meant so much to Rex! She just couldn't fail! Elaine frantically attempted to get back on course, but her gallant effort only made things worse. She didn't know how she ever managed to finish the song, but she felt frozen at its completion.

She stared out at the audience, crushed by the knowledge of how badly she had performed. She had failed them all, ruined the biggest show of the tour! Elaine's worst fears had been realized—a repeat of her childhood catastrophe, only this time before hundreds of people!

CHAPTER TWELVE

Elaine tried to maintain control. Despite the consequences, she must introduce her next song. She must go on, even though it might mean facing the biggest defeat of her life!

At that moment Rex appeared from the side-curtain. Levi followed him, stopping to speak to Oscar, then to Shelby. Rex moved over to the microphone to stand beside her. He flashed her a reassuring smile, speaking in his deep, confident voice.

"This next number is one Elaine just wrote. We are singing it tonight for the first time, 'The Glitter of the Road!'"

Backed by Levi, Denny, and Oscar's perfect music, Elaine felt her fears vanishing. In fact, the entire world receded, and only Rex and she existed. Rex stood close beside her. His nearness calmed her as their voices rose and blended, merging into one. Never before had she felt such complete freedom from self-consciousness. Rex, she, and the band were in total harmony, inseparable. She was lost in emotion caused by the beauty of the song, the thrill of singing with Rex.

They finished in perfect union the line Rex had helped her complete.

"And we will have each other, And the glitter of the road."

Then Rex stepped back leaving Elaine alone in the spotlight. The cheering crowd filled her with great elation. Elaine glanced at Rex and saw the triumph in his face.

With his arm clasped loosely around her waist, he announced, "Thank you very much. Elaine and I will be recording this in mid-September."

Elaine's last number, one she did alone, merited a standing ovation. The cheering went on and on. She glanced again at Rex. She owed her success, quickly snatched from failure, all to him. Rex had saved her performance tonight, just as last night he had saved her life.

"Great job!" Denny Mack said as they left the stage.

Rex was singing his final number, which was followed by the flash of cameras, the rush of enthusiastic autograph seekers. They were exhausted, but filled with the high of success, when the last of the crowd left and they stood alone in the great auditorium. Rex drew her into his arms and kissed her.

"Elaine, this is the happiest moment of my life!"

* * * *

Elaine, her world glowing, parted with Rex in the hotel lobby and continued up to her room. Her steps slowed as she approached the door. Someone had left her a note. She quickly unfolded the paper. Typed carefully in the center were the words, *I won't miss your next show*.

The magic of the evening abruptly drained away. Even though the message contained no stated threat, Elaine clearly understood its meaning. He—whoever he was—intended to strike again at their next performance!

With shaking hands she unlocked the door. The glaring, overhead lights did not seem to dispel the shadows. In them she envisioned Derrick, sullen and angry. Could he actually be carrying out some foolish plan to frighten her into leaving the tour?

Despite the late hour, Elaine dialed Derrick's number in New Orleans. The phone rang again and again, resounding and empty. More upset than before, she replaced the receiver and called The Highlands. Thad would surely have seen Derrick if he had gone back home after they had last talked.

The hour wasn't late, not for Thad, who often stayed at the club all night. Then why didn't he answer the phone? Feeling a growing sense of fear, Elaine re-read the words—*I won't miss your next show*. Nothing written here that she could take to the police. In fact, the message would sound totally innocent to anyone except her and Rex.

Thinking of Rex steadied her. She dialed his room. Evidently he was still downstairs. Too nervous to take the elevator, Elaine walked down the broad, winding stairway. The huge mirrors with their gilded-gold frames, the fabulous glass chandeliers, no longer looked magnificent to her.

She wandered through the vast area, looked into the

dining room and the lounge, then went outside and stood beside the decorative columns of the hotel. Heavy clouds filled with moisture hung low over the surrounding buildings and formed a dense fog over the parking lot. Elaine could make out the vague outline of the tour bus.

As she started toward it, the barely discernable form of a woman moved quickly away from the door. Elaine caught only a fleeting glimpse of black hair before the tall, slender figure disappeared into the mist. The short, dark hair, the proud set of her head and shoulders seemed familiar. Could Lisa Craft be here in Houston?

Music sounded from inside the bus. She had expected to find Rex, but Denny Mack admitted her, turning away to lower the volume of the tape player. On the table set a half-filled bottle of wine and two empty glasses.

"I thought I saw Lisa," Elaine said.

"Lisa Craft?" Denny gave a short laugh. "What would she be doing here? No, I imagine Lisa's right back in New Orleans running the company."

Elaine's gaze fell to the table.

"Who you saw was Mitzi. A fan of mine. Come to think about it, she does look a little like Lisa. Just not quite as flashy."

Denny's bold eyes traveled over Elaine.

"So, what brings you out here?"

"I'm looking for Rex."

"That's my luck. I thought you might be looking for me." He grinned and rubbed a hand across his reddish beard. "Care for a drink?"

Elaine shook her head, hand poised on the doorknob. Being out here alone with Denny made her uncomfortable.

Denny carried the wine and glasses over to the counter. When he turned back to her again, he said shortly, "Rex really came down hard on Shelby tonight."

"He has to learn to follow instructions."

Denny responded with an annoying arrogance. "People who make it big are never followers."

"But music takes discipline. Shelby will never survive in this business without it."

"Rex shouldn't put the boy down just because he's got spunk. No matter how hard Rex tries to make him a second, Shelby's headed straight for the top, just like me."

Elaine made no comment.

"It's not fair the way everyone blamed Shelby for those electrical problems."

"Someone deliberately tampered with the electricity," Elaine stated flatly.

"And you think they were out to get you." A slight, mocking smile tugged at the corners of Denny's lips. "Well, don't worry, honey."

Denny leaned back against the counter, watching her closely as if trying to gage her reaction.

"Rex was slated to go on first, not you."

"Who would want to harm Rex?"

"Someone with a lot to gain, I'd say."

"A take-over of Craft Music Productions, you mean," Elaine said. "The way I understand it, the partnership is in joint tendency. If something would happen to Rex, the business would belong totally to Lisa."

"On the other hand," Denny replied, "if something would happen to Lisa, Rex would own the company."

"Lisa's not in any danger."

"And neither is Rex. At least, not from Lisa. Theirs is an on-again, off-again relationship. But Rex and Lisa are two of a kind, a match made in 'heaven' for lack of a better word."

Elaine started to leave.

"Honey," Denny said, "even I can see how crazy you are about Rex. Being the good guy that I am, I'm going to warn you, even though you probably won't listen. Rex is just using you, exactly the way he uses everyone else. You're smack in the middle of a lover's quarrel. Rex is playing up to you just to make Lisa jealous so he can get her back."

Elaine's hand tightened on the door handle. "If Lisa is not trying to eliminate Rex to take over the company, then who did set up that 'accident' at Delta?"

Denny's answer, returned with the same candidness as her question, took her by surprise.

"You should take a good, close look at Oscar Macy."

"Rex and Oscar are the best of friends."

"They might have been once, but not after what Bill Craft did to Oscar. Oscar devoted his whole life to Craft Music Productions, then when the time came to sell out a partnership, Bill handed it over to Rex."

"But that's not reason enough to do all this."

"Knowing Oscar Macy, that would be justification

enough, but, of course, there could be more." A hard, brilliant glint appeared in Denny's eyes. "Oscar knows I'm on to him. Whatever he's doing, Elaine, I intend to find out. I'll bring him down, I'll promise the world that."

Elaine thought of Oscar's pleasant features, of his kindly smile. Denny had to be mistaken.

Denny continued as if to counter her unspoken opposition. "Oscar overheard a conversation Lisa and I had in Delta. We were discussing those threatening calls she's been receiving. She told you about them, I suppose."

"Yes."

"Lisa swears Oscar is the caller. She's familiar with the pretentious way he changes his voice, said it had to be him. I told her not to worry, Denny Mack thinks the same thing and is about to prove her right."

"But Oscar would never blame the company for a decision Bill Craft made."

"He's not blaming the company, honey. He's blaming Rex. Oscar is convinced that Rex plotted to turn Bill away from him and get the partnership for himself."

"Oscar wouldn't believe Rex capable of that."

"Wouldn't he? Underneath that big smile, Oscar hates Rex and would do anything to ruin him."

A chilling silence fell between them.

"Oscar pretends to be a clown," Denny said, "but really he's just a hateful, old man, filled to the brim with bitterness and spite."

CHAPTER THIRTEEN

Elaine gazed from the bus window where waves of heat drifted up from the hot pavement. She had told no one about the warning note she had received, but it still weighed heavily on her mind.

Except for Rex, everyone would simply believe the message had been written by a zealous fan that had missed the show. But Rex, if he knew, would read between the lines and insist that she return to New Orleans. And Elaine could not do that. She could not leave Rex now, not when his danger might be even greater than her own.

Elaine realized that her decision to remain silent vied against wisdom and common sense. Ever since the bus had pulled away from Houston, she had been gripped by a feeling of foreboding, warning that today's journey would be neither uneventful nor safe.

Nothing to base this fear on, she thought. Everything seemed ordinary, peaceful, even. Through the glass partition she could see Denny alone in the front, calmly intent on his driving, red hair aglow from the brilliant, slanting sunlight.

Elaine glanced around at her companions. After last night's success, everyone was basking in high spirits. Rex and Levi smiled as Oscar's bragging about the show became more exaggerated. Shelby, like a typical teenager, stretched out on the couch, sound asleep.

Soon Oscar rose, tapped on the partition, and called to Denny, "Oscar's turn to drive."

The bus pulled off the road and came to a bumpy stop. As Oscar and Denny changed places, Rex joined Elaine at the table. She cast a quick glance at him, wishing she could once again experience the jubilation she had felt singing with him last night, but try as she might, she could not share his carefree mood.

"Is something wrong, Elaine?"

Giving into an even greater sense of apprehension, she looked away, at the sweep of trees along the highway, and answered, "No, nothing's wrong."

As if in response to Elaine's words, Oscar's voice on the intercom announced, "My friends." He added with a deep chuckle, "My captives. We are not going directly to Padre Island, as planned. Solely for your pleasure and enjoyment we are making a side trip."

During a short pause he adjusted the microphone. "In case you haven't noticed, instead of continuing on Highway 59, we are proceeding north on 71. Your famous bus driver, *Macho* Macy, was born on a ranch northeast of El Campo, overlooking the glorious Colorado River." His deep voice gained volume. "Unfortunately the old home place, not faring as well as I, is little more than a ruin. But I am taking you to the exact spot of my roots so you might all contemplate my greatness."

The intercom sputtered and cracked as he replaced it.

"Rex, maybe we should just go directly to the island," Elaine said anxiously.

"Good call. But I'd have to fight Oscar over the steering wheel." Rex's smile lingered. "I'm not sure I'm up to that. You heard how he's beginning to call himself '*Macho* Macy.'"

Elaine, with a rush of concern over the detour, rose, and catching her balance from the sudden swaying of the bus, approached the partition.

"I would very much like to go straight to the hotel. Maybe we could drive out here later."

"Sorry, Elaine," Oscar replied. "I have this tugging in my heart strings today that pulls me off the main road." Oscar lifted the microphone again, his voice rising theatrically, "Voices are calling, 'Go home, Oscar, breathe the fresh air of the Colorado River valley. Renew your strength.'"

Elaine turned to Rex. "Is there some way...?"

"That I can silence the voices he hears?" Rex finished for her. "I'm afraid not." Rex's amused eyes met hers and remained on her as she returned to her seat.

Why was Oscar determined they make this side trip? As she gazed at Oscar Macy's broad back, she was filled with horror. What if Denny Mack's accusations had been right?

Her first impression, to trust Oscar Macy above the

others, now loomed as dead wrong. Oscar could be part of a conspiracy to take over this multimillion-dollar company. Levi or Lisa Craft could be taking advantage of Oscar's deep-seated resentment of Rex and might be making him a willing pawn in a get-rich-quick scheme.

Elaine looked out the window again. The day, so warm, so sunny and normal, seemed to make her fears and suspicions absurd. Her run-away thoughts had been prompted by that strange inner voice, like intuition, informing her of some fast-approaching disaster.

The flat land had some time ago become rolling hill country, spotted with ranches where herds of longhorn cattle grazed. Soon Oscar was certain to leave the highway and travel for perhaps miles back into the tree-filled valleys along the edge of the river. He would stop the bus in some unpopulated place where no help could be summoned. And then…what?

The disturbing visions had no sooner arisen in Elaine's imagination than the bus suddenly pulled on to an unkempt, dirt road that led farther and farther away from any inhabitants. Soon, it became only a narrow track that wound endlessly into the hills. She could feel the sudden jolts when the big wheels hit deep depressions.

"We have flash floods out here sometimes." Oscar's slow drawl, sounding over the intercom again, did nothing to allay her sense of unease. "These low sections of road fill up with water and become impassible."

"How much farther is it?" Rex asked, his voice toned to carry to the front seat.

"Five or six miles. It's beautiful country, you'll enjoy it. My favorite spot in this whole world is right out here, high on a cliff that overlooks the wide, deep Colorado."

"You're beginning to sound like a tour guide," Rex commented. "That's all right, unless you expect payment."

Elaine felt a tight clenching in her stomach, a reaction against their friendly banter. Rex continued to joke with Oscar, completely trusting, as if he had nothing at all to fear from this well-planned deviation from the normal route. And maybe he didn't. She had no evidence against Oscar Macy, only vague suspicions, most of which had their root in her talk last night with Denny Mack.

The road twisted upward through a tree-filled slope, which slowly leveled off into a flat plateau at a level base along the canyon. Elaine took a deep, steadying breath and tried to convince herself that worry and tension alone was causing her imagination to run wild.

The bus abruptly stopped.

"This is as far as we can go," Oscar called. "The road's impassable from here on, so from now on we're on foot."

Looking like a giant, he appeared at the side door.

"Everyone out! We're taking a little hike."

"It's too hot," Shelby groaned, stirring from his sleep.

"Don't give me any trouble," Oscar boomed. "This is a 'must-see.' I've driven way out here for the benefit of one and all."

Elaine hesitated. Rex rose and offered her his hand.

"We're already here. We have no choice but to be good sports."

To Elaine's surprise even Denny Mack joined them, although he and Shelby trailed a good distance behind.

"This road," Oscar explained, pointing to a scarcely visible trail overgrown with weeds, "will lead to the site of the old homestead. Some of the walls are still standing."

"We can't wait to see them," Rex joined in merrily, fully prepared to enjoy this unexpected outing.

During the long, difficult climb upward, Rex gripped Elaine's arm and pointed. "Look over there."

Elaine spotted an armadillo that had ventured from the seclusion of trees that no doubt harbored his grass-lined tunnel home. She watched as the scaled animal moved awkwardly along, snout to the ground, intent on his hunt for bugs. Suddenly, sniffing danger, he scuttled back into the cottonwoods.

In the interval of their pausing to watch the armadillo, Oscar, unmindful of the heat, had gained distance. Rex hurried to catch up, but Elaine halted uncertainly. She glanced back over her shoulder, but Denny and Shelby were no longer in sight. The vacant trail increased her fear. Knowing she couldn't remain behind and allow Rex and Oscar to go on alone, she hurried to catch up with them. Oscar, far in the lead, had side-tracked from the path toward a rock-lined ledge.

Against the backdrop of surrounding bluffs, the twisting Colorado River washed across beds of sheer stone. Directly below them the water dropped off and gathered into a deep, natural dam. Elaine shaded her eyes against the blinding sun, her gaze falling to the rocks and water so far below. The perfect place to stage another accident, she thought.

Oscar silently looked toward the flat grassland that sloped away from the rugged valley wall. He took off his hat and the wind ruffled his hair.

"This sight is what makes my tedious little life all worthwhile," he said, turning to face them. "Why are you standing so far back?" He gestured to them with a wave of his arm. "The good view's here. Move on up. Closer to me."

Shading her eyes, Elaine scanned the area ahead of them for signs of Oscar's old home. Her gaze lighted on ruined limestone walls that poked through the trees a safe distance away from the cliffs.

"I'm anxious to see where you lived. Let's go on."

"There's not much left of the old place," Oscar protested. "This is what I want you to see." Then he conceded. "All right, we'll go on. But first, let me take a photo."

Oscar reached for the strap he expected to be over his shoulder then said, "I left my camera back on the bus. I'll just go back after it."

Oscar had disappeared from view, before Rex exclaimed, "He'll never find his camera. He left it in the front seat, and I tucked it away under the couch."

Rex started after Oscar, his words floating back to Elaine, "You just wait here. I'll be right back."

Elaine considered following them, but reminded herself that Rex would be safe enough at the bus. If a disaster were planned, it would occur at this very spot, right on this cliff where she was standing.

The knowledge made her uneasy. She remained near the cliff for a long time, but they did not return. The waiting grew unbearable. At last she began climbing up the slope behind her, thinking at a higher elevation she would be able to see the bus or catch a sight of them somewhere on the trail.

She made her slow way upward through thick trees, high weeds, and sumac stalks. Total silence hung in thick layers as intense as the heat. The labored sound of her own breathing was broken suddenly by a scattering of stones and a loud, anguished cry.

Elaine froze. The tragedy she had feared from the moment she had boarded the bus had happened! A vision of Rex, falling, arose in her mind, then his form, limp and motionless sprawled at the base of the canyon. She heard herself shouting, "Rex!"

Barely aware of whirling around, Elaine ran, half-sliding, down the slope. She reached the overlook in seconds. The piercing cry sounded again, came from just over the rocky ledge beneath her. The dizzying height, the glare of the sun, made the form just below her wavy and uncertain. She couldn't identify the man clinging to the sheer side of the cliff, saw only broad shoulders and jean-clad legs. He clutched a stunted tree branch, boots scuffing against rock and earth in a frantic effort to seek some foothold.

Elaine dropped to the ground, flat on her stomach.

"Here! Try to reach my hand!"

She saw his features clearly as he looked up at her. Denny Mack! His pale skin was drenched with sweat, his eyes wide-open and frightened. His words rang out hoarsely. "I'll only drag you down with me!"

"You've got to try! See that rock just above you? It looks solid. Just grip my hand and use it as a brace."

Denny's indecision lasted far too long. His hold on the branch appeared to grow weaker by the moment.

"You've got to do this, Denny. You haven't any other choice!"

He let go of the branch and swung his hand upward. Elaine caught it with both of hers. His clutching fingers seemed to lack strength. His hand felt damp and slippery, but she held fast.

Rocks and sliding earth plummeted as he scampered upward, feet finding temporary support on the protruding rock. As he attempted to reach the stony edge, Elaine moved one hand to his arm and helped drag him up over the top.

He collapsed, panting, beside her on the ground.

"Oscar did this!"

"We should never have let him talk us into coming out here," Elaine said. "This place is so isolated. I was afraid someone might have an accident."

"Accident? This was no accident. That madman," Denny gasped, staring straight up at the sky. "That madman tried to kill me!"

CHAPTER FOURTEEN

Far below the sheer drop-off, jagged rocks lined the riverbank. First, the last minute diversion of a deadly electrical shock, next, the narrow escape of a fatal fall. Elaine shuddered as she turned back to Denny, still sprawled on the ground, eyes tightly closed. His large, white teeth clenched as if from a delayed reaction of fear or pain.

"Are you hurt?" Elaine asked, alarmed.

Her concern served to fully restore him, to cause his egotism to surface full force.

"Good thing I'm in A-1 shape."

Denny rose stiffly and began brushing at his clothes.

"It pays to work out. That's why I was able to grab that branch the way I did."

"I still don't understand," Elaine said. "Why are you so convinced Oscar was the one who pushed you?"

Denny answered with a question of his own. "Just why do you think he brought us out here today? I told you last night that he's afraid of me. It looks as if he wants to get me out of the way before he kills Rex."

In the stillness, Elaine could feel the pounding of her heart. Excited voices drifted to them, coming from the path that led to the bus. Rex reached them first, Levi and Shelby not far behind.

"We heard a cry," Rex said. "Did anyone get hurt? What's happened?"

"Denny almost fell from the cliff."

"Fell?" Denny snorted. "Tell them the truth, Elaine. I was pushed!"

"Ah, no one pushed you, Denny," Shelby spoke up.

The boy's words rang with an incredulous shrillness, yet he looked pale and shaken.

"You've been sipping too much out of that bottle you always carry. You probably just got too close to the edge and weaved right over."

"I thought you would be on my side," Denny said gruffly.

"You're just crazy. You probably got hit by some falling branch." Shelby didn't look at Denny as he spoke, instead skimmed the large tree above them for some sign of a broken limb.

"We've all been under a lot of pressure," Levi said. "That, and this heat causes imagination to run wild."

Only Rex seemed willing to take Denny's account seriously. He began to explore the area near the cliff, kneeling to examine a flattened place in the weeds.

"If someone did push you, we'll determine nothing from any of this," he said, "too many footprints here."

"I don't need any clues," Denny countered. "As you

can see, Macy's still hiding out. He's afraid to face me after what he just did."

"Oh, come to your senses, Denny," Levi said. "Oscar wouldn't do this. He wouldn't gain anything by killing you."

Shelby took a step closer to Denny. The boy wiped at his damp face with the back of his hand before asking in an appeasing way, "Did you actually see him?"

"I was struck from behind, Shelby. But I had the impression of height and weight. Besides that, I have other reasons to think Oscar pushed me. Personal ones. I want to talk to the sheriff."

"A real waste of time," Rex said.

Levi's eyes, steady and calm behind the dark-tinted glasses, leveled on Denny. "I wouldn't involve the law, but it's your decision, Denny. If that's what you want to do, I'll go back to the bus and make a call on the cell phone."

"You do that."

As they watched Levi walk away, oppressive silence closed over them, which Rex finally broke, "Just don't make any wild accusations, Denny."

"I might have known you'd try to protect Macy," Denny shot back. "But it's hard for me to see why. He's planned all this. He rigged the electricity in Delta to eliminate you. And he's dead-set on carrying this through to the finish."

Elaine felt the pounding of her heart increase. Rex's blue-black eyes, remote now, looked into Elaine's, but he did not speak.

"I don't like Oscar much, either," Shelby burst out. "But, remember, Oscar gave Rex his first break in the music business. You know what good friends they are. Why all of a sudden would he do something like this?"

"The guy's demented," Denny snapped back. "But I guess no one can see it but me. But if I were you, Rex, I'd be backing me up, I'd put Oscar Macy right in jail where he belongs."

At that moment Oscar appeared, breaking through trees and brush like some huge animal on a rampage. Once in the clearing, he stopped short. Breathing hard, he stood very straight and glared at Denny. The pleasant lines around his mouth sagged, his large eyes no longer bore that perpetual look of amusement. They gleamed icy and frightening.

Denny watched him warily.

Red blotches had formed on Oscar's face. They looked like colored pigments clinging to some weatherworn statue.

"Denny thinks someone tried to kill him."

Oscar remained glaring at Denny. "I just met Levi and he told me all about your little fall. He said you are accusing me of pushing you." Midway, Oscar's threatening tone changed, became pretentious and stagy. "As much as we'd all like to see you tumbling into the Colorado, I had no part in it."

Elaine noticed how Oscar often resorted to humor to camouflage his true feelings.

Oscar took a step closer to Denny, his tone becoming loud and aggressive. "And you had better not say I did unless you have the proof to back it up."

Denny drew forward, too.

Elaine, afraid that an all-out war would erupt between them, spoke the only words she could think of to distract them. "It wouldn't have to be one of us. Someone could have followed us here."

They both stopped and looked at her in surprise.

"You just tell the sheriff whatever you want to," Denny said, "and I'll do the same."

* * * *

Denny went into the bus. The others remained in a gloomy circle outside.

"Where were you at the time this happened?" Elaine asked Oscar.

"When I went back to the bus, I couldn't find my camera so I started back. Someone called my name. Whoever it was stood up on the hill above me. I thought it was you, Levi. But when I got to the top, I couldn't find anyone."

"No, it wasn't me. I took the shortcut directly to that old ruin of a house. What about you, Shelby?" Levi asked. "Where were you?"

Shelby averted his gaze.

"I don't know. I didn't want to see Oscar's house, so I was just out there wandering around."

"But you heard Denny yell?" Levi asked.

"Of course. Didn't everyone? I was just right above them. You saw where I was when I met you on the trail."

"I sure don't like this," Levi said. "I have a half a notion to tell the sheriff I was with you, Oscar. And save everyone a lot of pointless trouble."

"Thanks, old buddy," Oscar replied. "But, no, I don't want you to lie."

They could hear the distant sound of a motor before they saw the black vehicle kicking up swirls of dust. Denny must have heard it, too, for he came out of the bus and waited alertly.

A stocky man of about Oscar's age stepped out of the car marked Wharton County Sheriff's Department. He moved slowly, thick stomach stretching the limits of his khaki shirt. Like Oscar, even when serious, the impression of a smile remained on his lips.

Oscar's eyes lit up. "Not the Lone Ranger! Not Superman! But Sheriff Melvin Brady!"

The sheriff strode forward and clapped Oscar on the shoulder.

"I couldn't let anyone else handle this. When I heard there was trouble at the old Macy place, I set right out. After all, Oscar Macy is El Campo's very own celebrity!"

The sheriff's broad smile faded a little.

"Now, tell me, Oscar, just what's the trouble?"

Oscar pointed a finger at Denny. "This guy here thinks I tried to push him off a cliff."

"If you didn't push people off cliffs from time to time, what on earth would I have to do?"

Oscar joined the sheriff in his robust laughter.

Denny turned to Elaine. "An Oscar Macy clone," he said under his breath. "Just what we need." Then he swung back to the sheriff, demanding, "Are you going to make a report or not?"

Denny told Sheriff Brady what had happened and took him up to the place where he had fallen. When they returned, anxious to get out of the burning sun, the sheriff set up headquarters in the bus, using the table near the window as his desk. Then he asked to speak to each one of them in private.

When Elaine was called in, she mentioned at once the near disaster of their first show, the threatening phone call, and the note.

"Do you have any idea who's doing this?"

"No."

The sheriff shuffled through papers, then said, "Levi Culver thinks someone might be following the tour. This could be the work of some psycho, plenty of them around. Do you know of anyone who might have a grudge against you or against Denny Mack?"

"Not against me. I just started working for Craft Music Productions."

He remained silent for a while. "I find it odd," he said finally, "that no report was made in Delta."

"We had no proof that the electrical problem wasn't just an accident," Elaine replied.

"Just like today, there's still no proof."

"I have no doubt," Elaine said, "that both of these happenings were planned in advance and carefully carried out."

The sheriff tapped the point of his pen against the table

thoughtfully. "I've known Oscar Macy all my life. The idea that he's turned into a deranged killer is totally absurd."

Elaine did not know whether Oscar was a part of this or not, but she was beginning to believe that murder was not the motive behind these so-called accidents. That's why no one had really been harmed. They were merely a build-up, a scenario for the final kill, a murder to be blamed on to some innocent person, or to remain unsolved, the work of some crazy fan or rejected singer. A shiver crept down Elaine's spine.

The sheriff was watching her closely. "You have information that you're not telling me, don't you?"

She found herself repeating her thoughts aloud, "Whoever planned these accidents may not have had any intention of killing anyone. They may be setting the scene for their real victim."

"And that would be?"

"Rex Tobin."

After she explained to him why she believed the killer was after Rex, the sheriff said, "Could someone have mistaken Denny Mack for Rex Tobin today?"

True, they were about the same height and build. But Denny had been bareheaded today. His red hair, so different in color from Rex's, would have made such a mistake unlikely. "I don't think so."

The sheriff stood up and looked from the bus window. "Things look very bad," he said solemnly, "but what can I do? I'll write up a report, but I don't have evidence enough to detain Oscar Macy or anyone else. I'm totally without proof that a crime has even been committed."

With a stern warning for her to be careful, he gathered up his papers and stepped outside. The sheriff called a cordial goodbye to Oscar. "Everyone here loves your music. I'll be watching for your next CD."

The serious trouble for Oscar that Levi had anticipated had not occurred, but Rex had been right in his assessment—involving law enforcement had been a total waste of time. The sheriff had simply taken statements that would be filed away with other dead-end reports in some over-stuffed filing cabinet.

Rex had taken the wheel and Oscar, as if to get as far away from Denny as possible, rode up front beside him. Denny, moody and unapproachable, isolated himself near the back of the bus.

Elaine left the table to join him. To her surprise, Denny did not reject her effort at conversation.

"You saved my life," he said as she seated herself in a chair across from him. "I guess I owe you one."

Elaine noticed the solid tone of his muscular arms. If she hadn't appeared to help pull him up, he would, no doubt, have saved himself. But that didn't make what had almost happened to him any less serious.

Denny glanced toward the table where Levi and Shelby sat and said in a low voice, "I'm going to tell you something. This isn't over yet."

Denny's suspicions echoed her own.

"Strange things have taking place at CMP ever since Rex took over. The first chance I get, I'm going back to

New Orleans and see if I can get Lisa to confide in me. I intend to find out exactly what's going on. While I still can."

When they reached Victoria, Rex stopped the bus at a truck stop center near a bustling airport. "Anyone hungry?" he asked over the intercom, attempting to maintain a sense of normality.

The small group followed Rex into a spacious café. After Rex had settled at the table, he excused himself, saying, "Have to make a call."

Awkwardness followed Rex's departure. Elaine made small talk with Levi. Oscar and Denny did not look at one another, and Shelby kept shifting nervously in his chair, paying no attention to the menu he gripped so tightly.

Denny, eyes trained to the window, watched a big jet taxi into the runway.

Elaine was relieved when Rex returned.

"Just talked to Club Paradise," he said. "They want to reschedule our next show."

Levi looked up and said sharply, "That will be an expensive lay-over. I hope they intend to pick up the tab."

"Their grand opening was delayed, so that makes our next performance Saturday instead of tomorrow. We can all use a break. That leaves us with three days." Rex's eye caught Elaine's, and he tried to sound carefree and happy. "Three days on the beach with nothing to do but swim and relax."

"I'll be back for the next show," Denny said, suddenly rising to his feet. "But for now I'm out of here. I'm going over to that airport and see if I can catch a flight back to New Orleans."

"I'll walk over with you," Shelby volunteered. "But I don't know why you don't just go on with us to the island. We could spend some time working..." Shelby shot a sideways glance at Rex before finishing his sentence, "on our plans."

Denny ignored Shelby, who waited by his side like an eager pup. Instead, he told Elaine. "I have some important business—that won't wait."

"Monkey-business," Oscar drawled, turning around in his chair to watch Denny and Shelby depart.

CHAPTER FIFTEEN

At Aransas Pass, the bus was transported by ferry across the bay to Padre Island. Elaine stood at the railing watching the receding shoreline. If only she could rid herself of the fear that hovered over her like the gulls that swooped toward the boat.

"Tonight we've booked a hotel I approve of," Levi was saying. "The Sea Breeze is Padre Island's finest."

Wouldn't it be wonderful if everything were different, if she had carefree time to spend on the island with Rex? Elaine cast a glance at Rex's profile as he leaned close beside her, the sea breeze ruffling his dark hair.

"And it looks as if we're going to make an early arrival," Levi said as he gazed toward the fast-approaching dock.

After Elaine had settled into her room on the twelfth floor, she took out the threatening note, read, and reread the words, "I won't miss your next show." If Elaine were right, the "kill" that had been plotted from the beginning of the tour was to take place right on this island. Even with a three-day reprieve, she felt as if she were being propelled at whirlwind speed toward disaster.

But she wouldn't think of that now. Instead, she would take a walk by the ocean and breathe the fresh, salty air. Elaine stopped along the shore to watch a scattering of swimmers, then strolled on, trying to drive the dark thoughts from her mind. She soon found she had gone a good deal farther than she had thought. She stopped to look back toward the hotel, whose center rose to a majestic height, encircled by protective sidewalls that spread out in an eagle's pose, like the wings of some great, concrete bird.

She wandered on, past a young mother and her children gathering shells, past rock jetties, until she found herself on a lonely stretch of beach near a long, wooden pier. Although not a soul was in sight, as Elaine slipped off her sandals, she noticed a pair of men's shoes lying near the supporting posts.

Elaine waded through the shallow water in search of shells, enjoying the feel of sand beneath her bare feet. Soon, in the distance, she made out a lone form whose steps increased as she turned and shaded her eyes against the glare of sunlight. Rex! His white shirt, open at the neck, contrasted against his tanned skin. The legs of his rolled pants were damp and his feet were bare.

They were alike, both able to temporally abandon burdens and fears, like shoes, and walk away free, lost in the beauty of sky and choppy sea.

Rex hurriedly closed the space that separated them.

"I couldn't resist the temptation to come out here," he

said, as if feeling guilty for putting pleasure before business.

"Neither could I."

Rex caught her hands and smiled at her. The sea breeze billowed his shirt and hair, and sparkles of light blended with the dark blue depths of his eyes.

As they walked on down the beach, Elaine would hold up shells for his inspection, and many would meet with a laughing rejection and a toss into the ocean. Rex bent to gather up pieces of a sand dollar.

"Broken," he said with disappointment. "Sand dollars are what you see most of out here. But perfect ones are hard to find."

At that moment Elaine found one. Rex took the sand dollar from her hand and studied its smooth, round shape.

"Perfect!" he pronounced in amazement. "Be careful," he cautioned as Elaine placed it gently into her shirt pocket. "They are so easy to break."

Elaine felt totally immersed in the moment—the vast shoreline, the roaring sea.

All too soon, Rex glanced at his watch and said reluctantly, "I have to go back to the hotel now. Business meeting."

He works too hard, Elaine thought, pushes himself too much.

"I'm going back now, too," Elaine said. "I need to work on my compositions."

Rex's fingers closed around hers as they strolled hand in hand back to the hotel.

As they parted in the lobby, Rex asked, "Elaine, would you have dinner with me tonight?"

* * * *

Back in her room, Elaine worked on her music for several hours but finished far too early to get ready for her seven-o'clock date. Wanting to shake the gloom that had crept back into her thoughts, she decided to go once again to the beach. Silly, she thought, to think that she would encounter Rex in the exact same spot she had found him earlier. Still, feeling like a schoolgirl, she clung to the hope of another chance meeting.

Elaine hadn't gone far when she got the sensation that someone was following her. She turned around, half-expecting to see Rex, but no one was in sight. At another time her pause to look back would have been only to absorb the beauty of white-capped waves rolling over the sandy shoreline. But now she felt gripped by a sudden fear, by an acute awareness of being watched.

Elaine's gaze moved from the vast and empty space directly behind her toward the abrupt rise of sand dunes. If someone were following her, he was edging his way through that rough, sloping ground and had ducked out of sight the moment she had turned. Was he waiting for the opportunity to catch her alone and defenseless?

A warning flashed though Elaine's mind to return to the hotel. But she was by now just as close to one of the jetties where several men were fishing.

She pressed on. Just as she reached her destination, a lean figure in faded T-shirt and jeans crossed from the sand dunes to sink down beneath the shade of the wooden pier. With relief she recognized Shelby. Surely he had been the one trailing along behind her. She watched as he, thin frame hunched, leaned back against the pier's wet wooden beam.

As Elaine drew closer, she saw that he was writing in a notebook. She hesitated a moment before silently approaching and taking a seat beside him on the sand. For a while both of them watched the high waves strike the shoreline and creep closer, almost intruding on their chosen spot.

"When I was a girl, my father used to take me out on a boat along the bayou. That's where I wrote the lyrics to my first song."

Shelby said nothing.

"I feel the same sense of inspiration here," Elaine said. "Isn't the sea beautiful?"

Shelby tossed back windswept hair. "I'm not really writing a song, just impressions."

He still did not look at her. She waited, her own gaze on the ocean.

After a while, Shelby, as if he were a little embarrassed, said, "I'm trying to put down how the water looks in the sunlight."

"How does it look to you?"

Very seriously Shelby studied his notes.

"Waves the color of gunmetal, tinged with shimmers of light." He pointed as he spoke, "See that streak of almost-pink in the clouds? I don't see how anyone could ever describe that."

Elaine was beginning to see that sensitive side to Shelby that he so seldom revealed. She looked up at dusky brushes of rose and coral in the horizon. No written words could ever capture that special blend of color.

"The inadequacy of words, that's the curse of the poet."

"I'm not a poet."

"Song writers are poets, too. But all we can do is try to record our feelings the best we can."

"Rex is never satisfied with anything I do," Shelby said suddenly. "He's just like Mom and my step-dad, and all the others. I can't do anything to please any of them. Except for Denny," Shelby's voice rose a little. "But it looks as if I'm even wrong about him."

Elaine, having just lost her own father, knew what it was like to be alone. She understood Shelby's pain. Added to it now was Denny Mack's abandonment, smoldering, no doubt, because Shelby had chosen to stay with the tour instead of going off with him.

"I know you're wrong about Rex," Elaine said.

"He's always angry with me."

"Often the people who care about us the most seem the most judgmental."

"Rex doesn't really care about me. He'll be glad enough to get rid of me. I can't wait to break away. If Denny won't go with me, I'll go alone. I'll form my own band. Here, I'm just in the way."

"I really wish you would stay."

Shelby's long dark hair blew in a sudden gust of wind. He looked very young and vulnerable.

"Even after I messed up your song like that?"

"Just an error in judgment. Perfectly forgivable. Shelby, whether you know it or not, Rex is on your side."

"You know, maybe I would stay if Rex asked me to." His voice died away.

"But he won't. Because he really doesn't care. Just like Mom, he'll be glad enough to be shed of me."

"If that's what you really want, Shelby, then I hope Denny and you can work together, start your own show."

"I tried to talk to Denny about our plans when I walked with him to the airport this morning, but he didn't even seem interested. I even followed him to the boarding gate."

Shelby turned to her with a frown.

"But do you want to know something strange? I didn't see Denny get on the plane."

Shelby's words stayed with Elaine. Once back in her room again, she, on impulse, placed a call to New Orleans. A cool, pleasant voice answered.

"Craft Music Productions. Lisa Craft."

"I would like to speak to Denny Mack."

A hesitation followed

"He just left. Whom shall I say called?"

"Elaine Sands. I just wanted to ask Denny if he would trade places with me on Saturday night's show. I would like to go on before Rex."

"He probably won't be back in the office until tomorrow. But I'll tell him the minute he comes in."

"I'm not even sure Denny planned on re-joining the tour," Elaine said, then went on hurriedly, "I suppose he told you all about what happened in El Campo."

"Denny refuses to trust any official at Crafts'," Lisa replied, "Oscar Macy, in particular." She gave a little sigh. "I only hope it doesn't turn out to be one of our employees."

"So do I."

"Elaine, Thad was just here gathering up your father's work. Are you dead certain about this refusal to sell?"

"Yes."

Lisa's voice took on an edge.

"Since you're working for us now, I thought that might make a difference to you."

"Why would it?"

"I'm going to speak frankly, Elaine. The company is in very serious trouble. If we don't do something quickly, manage to turn things around, we might not have anything left to salvage. I think your father's songs might be the answer, might give us the hit album we need."

Elaine remained silent.

"Rex will record them. You wouldn't mind that, would you?"

"Not if I wanted to sell them."

"I'm not blaming anyone for the company's problems," Lisa went on, "but ever since Rex became my partner and Levi took over the accounting, we've been on a steady downhill course. Denny's convinced there's something amiss. In fact, the minute he got here, he insisted that I arrange for a complete audit of the books."

CHAPTER SIXTEEN

Ripples of fast-fading light angled across sand and water as Rex and Elaine left the hotel for dinner.

"I know of a little restaurant down by the pier that serves the island's finest seafood."

Despite the gathering darkness, hotel guests lounged in chairs, played in the surf, strolled, as Rex and Elaine were doing, along the ocean-front walkway.

"I always enjoy this part of the tour best," Rex said. "By this time the toughest gig, Houston, is behind us and from here on it's smooth sailing."

If only that were true. Elaine thought of the note she had brought along to show Rex, of its terrible implications. But she did not want to ruin the evening from the very start. They walked on, with only the pleasant sound of waves breaking against the shore.

Once they had arrived at the restaurant, Elaine could not help glancing behind them. A couple walked hand in hand, a group of yelling teenagers tossed a beach ball—nothing threatening or in the least bit suspicious. Then why did she feel so uneasy?

"Are you looking for someone?" Rex asked.

Elaine mustn't let the fear and pressure that had been building up for the past few days ruin this evening, their first real date. She smiled at him.

"No, I'm just enjoying the scenery."

The restaurant set high on stilts. They sat near the huge window that overlooked the ocean. Above them a net, overflowing with shells, hung low from the ceiling. The glowing candle on their table cast flickering light into the dimness, deepening and enhancing Rex's features, the masculine lines of broad forehead, high cheekbones, and well-defined lips. His black hair curled from moisture, and his eyes seemed deeper, warmer than tropical water.

But instead of enjoying their time alone, Elaine began to feel an ever-increasing apprehension. Her eyes strayed from Rex's face. Just beyond the window, still in her view, waves pelted the shoreline. Night and mist added a dimension of eeriness. Elaine suddenly caught a quick movement. A dark form, a moment ago immobile, slipped away, surreptitiously blending into the darkness. Someone *had* followed them, had been lurking just outside the cafe, watching them! She drew in her breath.

"What is it, Elaine?"

Rex looked from the window, too. She was beginning to read catastrophe into every common happening. The image just beyond the glass must be simply an innocent tourist deciding whether or not to have dinner here.

"Nothing."

Elaine focused her attention back to Rex and smiled. The stealthy form, however, remained imprinted in her thoughts, made her aware of danger just as she was aware of the crashing force of the ocean waves beyond the window.

Her tension began to ease during the progression of the meal. Rex was recalling incidents from his past tours that made her laugh. They lingered over fresh salad, baked potatoes and shrimp, breaded to perfection, served with a spicy cocktail sauce. She discovered that they had so much in common besides a love of music and the bayou country.

Elaine accepted a second cup of coffee, wanting their special evening together to last as long as possible. She even felt close enough to Rex to talk to him about Shelby.

"I spoke to Shelby this afternoon," she said.

"So did I. Against my better judgment, I agreed to let him go back on stage. Not that the concession did anything to endear me to him. No matter what I say or do, Shelby remains rebellious."

The sudden sadness that darkened Rex's eyes told Elaine how much this wayward nephew must mean to him.

"I just can't seem to battle Denny Mack's influence."

"Denny does all he can to cause trouble for you. I often wonder why you keep him on."

"Because Denny is a first-rate singer. And I do believe he sees potential in Shelby and wants him to succeed as much as I do. Speaking of Denny, he called and asked me to pick him up at the airport tomorrow morning at nine. Levi's got the bus tied up, so I rented a car. I'd like you to go with me. After we drop Denny back here, I'll show you around the island."

"Yes, I'd love to go."

Rex smiled.

"This is the first call I've ever got from Denny. Do you suppose he's starting to feel guilty for turning Shelby against me?"

"I think I'm the one to blame for your latest trouble with Shelby."

Rex reached out and covered her hand with his.

"You don't need to blame yourself, Elaine. Our problems started a long time ago. I guess I try too hard to be the father figure he needs so badly and that's why he resents me so much. My brother, John, and I were very close, and I find myself attempting to fill in for him. But I'm beginning to think it was a mistake dragging Shelby along this summer against his will."

Elaine knew that despite Rex's words, he wasn't sorry Shelby was here, and he was as determined as ever to keep the boy out of trouble. Elaine promised herself she would make an effort to befriend the sullen teenager and do all she could to try to ease the friction between Rex and him.

Elaine had postponed showing Rex the note as long as she could. Now, after what had happened to Denny, she knew for his safety and that of the entire band, she must share everything she knew with him. Dreading his reaction, she simply passed the message across the table.

"I found this slipped under my door after our last show."

She studied Rex, determining that he read the same warning into the words as she did.

"I was so certain that I was the one targeted by that so-called accident in Delta!" Rex said angrily. "But after what happened at El Campo and now this, I'm no longer sure of anything."

"Did Lisa tell you about the threats she received?"

He hesitated. "Yes, she did. This happens in the music business more often than you'd think. Being in the spotlight sometimes attracts unstable fans. But when Lisa left the tour, I believed she was overreacting. Now I'm beginning to think Lisa may have been right—there's some crazy person out there with a grudge, not only against her, but against the entire company."

"I don't think so, Rex."

"Then what do you think, Elaine?"

"I think someone pushed Denny to disguise the motive for his real target, which is either you or me."

"Surely, you can't believe someone plans to kill you."

Rex's reaction of astonishment faded, and he looked closely at Elaine as if for the first time he was taking this idea seriously.

"Is there anyone who would gain by your death?"

Elaine did not mention Thad, who was her natural heir. She thought briefly of her father's songs, but Thad would never kill her to own them.

"No one would."

"What about that fellow with you at the audition, Derrick Kline?"

She thought about Derrick's being backstage that night in Delta. But Derrick couldn't have been angry enough either at her or Rex to plot such deadly revenge.

"I've known Derrick a long time," Elaine said finally.

Convinced he had exhausted all possibilities, Rex said, "Then it is more logical to assume these threats are directed at me, not you."

"I believe you're right, Rex. You're the one in danger."

"Whatever the case," Rex said firmly, "I want you to quit the show, to go back to New Orleans."

She had known this would be his conclusion.

"Don't ask me to, Rex. I won't even consider leaving."

"This is not a game, Elaine. It's for real. No matter what the motive, all of us are in danger. Someone is likely to get hurt. And I'm not going to let it be you."

"I'm staying right here."

Rex kept insisting and Elaine remained adamant. Soon he fell silent as if the last word had not been said.

As they left the restaurant, Elaine felt a sudden reluctance to start the long walk back across the empty beach to the hotel. But once outside the freshness of the air, so heavy with salt and water, and the roaring of the sea served to steady her. Or was it Rex's tall, muscular form beside her, his hand tightly holding hers?

The lights of the hotel grew steadily closer, although they walked very slowly, feet sinking into the sand. Rex suddenly stopped and gazed out at the rolling surf. Elaine stood beside him, and for a moment they watched the lights of a distant ship play against the water.

"It's so beautiful out here, so peaceful." Elaine said.

Elaine caught her breath as Rex gently drew her into his arms. She closed her eyes and clung to him, fingers intermingled with the ocean-dampness of his hair. Their lips met, and the world seemed to melt away at the touch of his lips.

"I won't let anything happen to you, Elaine. I'm falling in love with you."

Try as she would, Elaine couldn't sleep that night. She ended up standing on the hotel balcony, twelve stories above the parking lot, clutching the wrought-iron railing. The cool, salty ocean breeze swept at her hair and clothing. She couldn't get Rex out of her mind, his words, the touch of his lips. Elaine Sands, content to be alone and independent, was actually falling in love, was actually counting the minutes until she could see Rex again.

She looked down to the dimly-lit parking lot so far below, her attention caught by the movement of a flashlight. She made out the figure of a man leaning under the open hood of a small car. Someone having car trouble, no doubt. As the form straightened, she caught a glimmer of silver from the man's hatband.

The dark hat with its silver band made Elaine think of the hat Rex had bought after their first show. Maybe it was Rex, checking out the rental car they would take to the airport tomorrow. She wanted to call his name, but didn't, merely watched him slam down the hood of the car and disappear into the darkness.

CHAPTER SEVENTEEN

Rex was waiting for Elaine in the lobby the next morning. She could tell by his preoccupied manner that something was wrong.

"I'm expecting an important visitor from Austin. He's going to detain me here for the rest of the morning. I hate to keep Denny waiting. Could you do me a favor, Elaine? Would you pick Denny up at the airport?"

"Of course."

"Thanks."

With a relieved look, Rex pressed a set of keys in her hands.

"The rental car is just out front, a blue Toyota. I'll walk out with you, show you where it's parked. I'm so sorry about this."

"I don't mind, Rex."

As Elaine slipped into the Toyota, she glanced up toward the balcony where she had stood last night. Rex lingered as if he wanted to delay as long as possible their moment of parting.

"I'll make this up to you," he promised. "We'll have

lunch when you get back then tour the island."

Leaning through the open window to kiss her, he cautioned, "Traffic is bad this time of morning. Drive carefully, Darling."

Elaine reached the highway and looked back to see Rex, the ocean breeze tugging at his shirt, still watching her. Feeling lonely without him, she headed down the long stretch of road that followed the island's gray waterfront. She soon reached the long, high bridge that arched over the gulf, connecting the island with the mainland.

It must be nearing eight o'clock, she thought, surprised at the steady flow of traffic. She pulled into the long line of commuters, her eyes skimming the warning sign: No Passing on Bridge. Elaine gave her brakes a light tap. Frowning, she noticed that it took more pressure than she had expected to slow the little car. In fact, she found herself inches away from the bumper of the red truck just ahead.

Elaine would have enjoyed the view from the bridge, the dazzling drop to bay water so far below, if not for the bumper-to-bumper traffic. The steady stream of vehicles forced her up the steep incline much faster than she liked to drive. The crowded bridge, a car she was not accustomed to driving, made her feel a tensing of the muscles across her neck and shoulders.

Some kind of congestion up ahead—road construction on the opposite side of the bridge—had caused the fast-moving chain of cars to slow unexpectedly. Elaine started to apply her brakes but felt only the spongy giving of the pedal beneath her foot. The blue rental car surged forward, dangerously close to the bumper ahead.

Anxiously, she pumped harder. Nothing happened. Elaine leaned forward tensely, her foot slamming against the brake pedal. With a feeling of sinking dread, she realized that the brakes were not working!

She couldn't turn back because of the rapid flow of traffic behind her. As fast as she was driving, she would soon reach the summit of the bridge and the car was certain to go out of control on the downward slope! Frantically she turned off the ignition. The car, even without acceleration, sped along.

Elaine started the precarious descent. She now faced a life-or-death decision. She must either collide with the car in front of her or take a chance and pull into the other lane! With split-second action, Elaine swung her vehicle recklessly around the Honda. She found herself face to face with a van heading straight toward her with relentless swiftness. The driver—she could see his startled face—reacted with great skill. With a screech, his van veered, skidding dangerously close to the side of the bridge.

Elaine's heart pounded. Time became suspended. She could not take her eyes from the road, but she heard no crunch of steel against metal guards, only the angry blasting of horns. With wet and shaking hands she continued steering wildly from lane to lane, through unbelievably narrow gaps in the traffic.

Panic, threatening to overtake her, sapped the strength from her limbs. She was never going to make it alive to the end of the bridge! The car, totally out of control, continued to pick up speed on the straight-down descent! One wrong decision would mean certain death!

Terrifying visions flashed rapidly through her mind. She pictured herself crashing headlong into another vehicle and being hurled into deep, icy water so far below!

She could manage the Toyota no longer. It raced downward at roller-coaster speed. Stopping the runaway car without causing a collision posed as much danger as the mad race across the bridge. Realizing she must find a way to get out of the mainstream of traffic, Elaine searched desperately for a place to turn off. Successfully guiding the car to a safe stopping place was her only hope of avoiding disaster!

Just ahead, she caught sight of a blocked-off ramp that led to a dirt road that wound under the bridge. Bracing herself, ignoring the bright orange construction signs and barricaded entrance, she turned into the closed exit. Orange barrels scattered as the car sliced through a gate-like barrier and began to tear down the winding, unpaved track. Up ahead, blocking the way, loomed a piece of heavy construction equipment. Unable to steer out of the way, Elaine could only cry out in horror as the car becoming slower and slower settled to a stop just inches from the gigantic bulldozer. Elaine slumped limply over the steering wheel and closed her eyes.

At last, feeling weak and shaken, Elaine stepped from the Toyota and surveyed the damage caused by crashing through the wooden blockade. The car had only a few minor scrapes and dents. She listened to the roar of overhead traffic from the bridge above. She knew that being able to steer the car into this blocked-off construction exit was all that had saved her! She shuddered at the thought of what might have happened if she had been compelled to continue on the highway, straight into the one-way traffic caused by the road repairs.

The car sat at an angle at the edge of a deserted construction site. A cement mixer and heavy yellow crane rose like prehistoric monsters from mounds of bare dirt. Just beyond the construction equipment, along the gray edges of the shore she identified what looked like a bait shop. She could see glimpses of the sprawling concrete buildings that marked the outer edges of the city limits. They were much too far away. She set out, oblivious to the sandy dirt in her shoes, toward the bait shop.

Seeing that she was stranded, the man behind the counter readily offered her the use of his phone. Elaine found the number and called the rental agent.

"I've been in an accident in one of your rental cars," she said, trying to keep her voice calm.

"Are you injured?" the very formal, female voice inquired.

"No, just shaken, and luckily the damage to the car is minimal."

"How did it happen? Was another vehicle involved?"

"No. I was crossing the bridge when the brakes on the car suddenly quit working. I had to exit into a construction site. That's what caused the damage."

The full impact of what had just happened suddenly

sinking in caused Elaine to break out in a cold sweat.

"I could have been killed," she said.

The voice turned dubious, a little defensive. "Our mechanics check every car thoroughly before it is rented. Each vehicle we rent is in perfect condition. I'll notify the police and we will take care of the car. You must stay where you are until an accident report is made."

After she had given directions, Elaine replaced the phone. A slowly spreading fear reached the pit of her stomach, making her feel very ill. This had been no accident!

The shadowy figure, the raised hood of the car in the parking lot now took on sinister meaning.

Last night someone had tampered with the brakes of this car, the same person who had planned and carefully set the stage for an electrical disaster at Delta, the same person who had pushed Denny Mack. She had not seen his face, had caught only a glimpse of dark hat and silver hatband—a hat that looked exactly like the one that belonged to Rex.

CHAPTER EIGHTEEN

Oscar, white Stetson pulled back revealing his mass of grayish hair, stood like a guard in front of the Sea Breeze Hotel. At the first glimpse of the taxi, he strode forward to meet Elaine.

"I've been worried about you. Denny came back in a cab a while ago. He said you never met him at the airport."

Still feeling jittery, Elaine told him the details of the near-accident.

"Where's Rex?" she ended up asking.

"A car came by and picked him up, some big meeting about a recording contract. He told me to apologize to you and tell you he won't be back until very late."

As Oscar spoke, his firm hand on her arm guided her into a back booth in the hotel's cafe. "Let me buy you a cup of coffee."

Once seated across from him, Elaine noted a deepening of his frown.

"Rex needs to know about this," he said. "I'll keep a look-out for him. He's set up a little office in the annex behind the hotel. He'll return there sometime this evening." Oscar stopped short, then said grimly, "One accident is believable. But more than one can't be just a coincidence."

"I saw someone in the parking lot tampering with the car last night," Elaine said. "I didn't think anything of it until after what happened."

"Sounds to me as if someone might have cut the brake line so the fluid would leak out. Rex told me last night the two of you were going to the airport after Denny. News gets around. One thing's clear, whoever jimmied those brakes doesn't mind harming you to get to Rex."

Elaine took a bracing sip of coffee. The impact of his words made her hands tremble. She considered telling Oscar about the glimpse of silver hatband, about the horrible thought that kept arising, that she had seen Rex last night tampering with the car. She decided against it. A quick glimpse of a dark hat with a silver band was not proof of anyone's guilt.

She told Oscar about the note she had received in Houston. "Whoever is doing this will be certain to strike again at our next show. I'm afraid of what's going to happen."

"Rex has no choice but to let you go on," Oscar replied, "They booked the show in the first place because of Lisa. They'll expect a female singer. But, don't worry, Elaine, I'll be keeping watch."

For what good that would do, Elaine thought.

"If Denny Mack hadn't been in New Orleans last night," Oscar said, "I would be thinking he was behind this."

"But Denny was almost a victim himself," Elaine replied. "Besides, Denny wouldn't have much to gain by killing Rex."

Oscar leaned forward and spoke with great feeling. "You don't know what it's like to have another man step in and get what you want, to crush a whole lifetime of dreams!"

Was he talking about Denny or himself and the partnership Bill Craft had given, not to him, but to Rex? As Elaine gazed at his rock-hard features, she felt she had for an instant broken through Oscar's pleasant facade and collided with the bitterness Denny Mack had insisted was there. The realization startled her.

"You've seen how Denny makes a little god out of himself," Oscar said with great animosity. "When Bill ran the company, Denny was the undisputed star."

For a long while Oscar remained solemnly quiet.

"His rivalry with Rex has become an obsession. He blames Rex alone for his being confined permanently to past tense."

Oscar's voice became pretentious, theatrical, as it often did when he was clowning. In spite of the comic effect, his words sounded stilted and humorless.

"A lot of malice exists in Denny Mack's ugly heart! Enough to want Rex Tobin dead!"

Elaine shivered. It was almost as if Oscar were speaking through Denny as a ventriloquist talks through a dummy, using him as a means to vent his own deep-seated resentment.

"Wanting is one thing, cold-blooded murder is another." Elaine said. "Whoever is behind this must plan to gain more than petty revenge."

"Money, you mean?"

Remembering what Lisa had told her about the book audit, she asked suddenly, "Does Denny handle any of CMP's funds?"

"Not on your life. Levi is in full charge of accounting. Both Lisa and Rex go through Levi to spend company money."

"Oscar, is Craft Productions in deep financial trouble?"

Oscar hesitated.

"Levi's after both Lisa and Rex for over-spending, but that's Levi for you. He watches expenditures like an eagle watches prey."

Oscar took a sip of coffee.

"No, I think the company's sound. I believe you're on the wrong track."

He paused, studying Elaine for a long time before he asked, "So, who's in line to inherit the Sands fortune?"

Elaine called nothing her own, but debts and her father's unsold songs. She attempted a smile.

"No suspects. No fortune."

* * * *

Gusts of wind swirled the sand on the beach, and the overcast sky looked somber and threatening. Whether she wanted to or not, Elaine must talk to Rex the moment he returned. She intended to tell him what she hadn't told Oscar, about the glint of silver on the hatband she had seen.

She hoped she would be able to judge from his reaction whether or not he had intentionally allowed her to go alone to the airport to pick up Denny Mack, whether he had purposely stayed away from the hotel when the news of the accident came. She spent most of the day inside waiting anxiously for Rex to return. She rang his room from time to time, but no one answered.

Evening would soon fall. He must be back by now. Remembering what Oscar had said about Rex's using a room in the hotel annex for an office, she took the elevator to the bottom floor.

A tropical storm was sweeping in from over the Gulf. Elaine left the hotel and passed a garden and empty pool. This late in the day, the stucco building, which housed a private conference area and several business suites, looked totally deserted. She reached the entrance and hurried to take cover from the sudden, pelting rain.

To her relief, Rex had returned. From the open door of the first office, she could see his dark hair and broad shoulders. In his well-cut suit, he looked more like a businessman than a singer. He sat behind a desk, a phone receiver clutched tensely in his hand as he leaned forward.

Not wanting to disturb him, Elaine began to walk silently toward him. The sound of her name being spoken made her stop in her tracks as quickly as if a shot had been fired.

"Don't worry. I'll take care of Elaine."

Silence hung heavily as Rex listened to the voice on the other end of the line, interrupting only once to say, "You had better leave right away, Lisa, if you plan to arrive before the show."

Elaine drew in her breath. Rex was talking to Lisa Craft. They were discussing her and Saturday's performance.

"Then it's all settled. You'll be on hand to take Elaine's place. You catch a flight as soon as you can. I'll handle the rest."

Rex listened again. When he spoke this time, irritation sounded in his voice.

"Of course you have to. You want your share of the profit, that means you have to take your share of responsibility. You're involved in this, too, you know."

Involved in what? Was Rex referring to their company or their plot to gain control of her father's songs? Elaine edged back to the entrance and slipped noiselessly out into the hallway.

Rain was beating down in torrents as she left the building. She was drenched in a second, clothes clinging miserably to her. She felt choked by the rain and wind and barely able to breathe. She began half-running, totally unmindful of the pools of water that splashed at her every step.

Once inside her room, Elaine crossed to the window and watched the streams of water pouring against the glass doors of the balcony. She tried to convince herself that Rex's talk with Lisa didn't have to mean that the two of them had planned these accidents, that they were partners, plotting together for the survival of their company.

Yet the alternative was equally devastating—Rex was in love with Lisa. He must know enough about what was going on to realize that Lisa would be safe. He was deliberately making use of an opportunity that would force Lisa to return to the show and to him. Denny Mack had clearly warned her that Rex was using her, a pawn in some game to get Lisa back.

How could she have been so taken in by him? Elaine turned, her gaze falling to the denim shirt she had worn to the beach, which still hung over the chair. As if to convince herself that the magic time with Rex had really happened, she reached into the pocket for the sand dollar she had so carefully placed there. At least she had this keepsake, a symbol of her momentary happiness.

Elaine held it in her hand, only to find that it had cracked into several pieces. As she tried to fit together the parts, they crumbled into sand. Tears filled her eyes. Sand dollars, like hearts, were so easily broken.

Wet and shivering, Elaine sank across the bed and cried.

She cried for Dad and the old days when music had been a golden, faraway dream, a joy. She cried because she felt betrayed by the only man she had ever loved. She cried because she felt totally defeated, lonelier than she had ever felt in her life.

CHAPTER NINETEEN

Why hadn't Elaine followed Derrick's advice and stayed in New Orleans? How she would welcome the sight of The Highlands now and of Thad, the friend she had always turned to when things went wrong. She forced herself to sit upright, to fight against her terrible sense of despair.

At first she had been angry at Thad for taking her father's songs without telling her. Now she began to feel sorry over the rift between them. No doubt, Thad thought a lifetime of support and loyalty had given him the right to do what he had done.

Elaine did not reach for the phone, but remained near it. Thad had always been a part of her and Dad's life, through both good times and bad. She remembered how he had looked in the hospital when she had watched him intercept the doctor the night of her father's last illness.

"Are you his son?" the doctor had asked.

Tearful and choked, Thad had not been able to reply.

"We did all we could. Mr. Sands didn't make it through the operation."

Thad's devotion to her father, Thad's unwavering belief in him, had never waned. Elaine wondered how she could have doubted Thad's motives, for she knew he had transferred this same caring affection to her.

She rang the club.

"Thad, I just wanted to talk to you."

"I'm surprised. I was afraid you'd still be upset with me."

His voice was toned lower than usual, with an unfamiliar ring of dejection. "I know I was wrong going behind your back and trying to sell Uncle Steven's songs without getting your permission. But it was your interests I had in mind, not mine or theirs."

"I know."

Thad's tone grew immediately lighter. "I would have given anything to have been in Houston. I saw your photo in the paper, singing your song, 'The Glitter of the Road,' with Rex. You looked just like I knew you would in that blue dress—like an angel."

"I wish you had been there, too, Thad."

"I've been trying to call you," Thad said, his tone serious again. "When I was at Crafts yesterday, Lisa told me about what's been happening. I think you're in real danger, Elaine. You've got to quit the tour and return to New Orleans."

She tried to reply lightly, "Wasn't it you who said singing with Rex was going to make my career sky-rocket?"

"Only if you're alive to enjoy it."

Elaine, anxious to change the subject, asked, "Have you

seen anything of Derrick?"

"The last time I saw him, two or three days ago, he was acting crazy. He told me he was going to catch up with your tour. Didn't he?"

Elaine thought of the form lurking in the shadows outside the restaurant where she had dined with Rex, of the eyes that she had been so certain were watching her.

"I haven't seen him."

Thad drew in his breath sharply before he spoke. "You may have made a big mistake joining this tour. It looks to me as if something fishy is going on, and you're right in the middle of it." Thad went on hurriedly, "It sounds to me as if Lisa Craft is back here hiding while you're on the front line. Your safety is what's important, Elaine. For your own good, you've just got to get out. Now."

Thad's warning hung heavily into the silence. She knew how Thad would look, sitting in his office, surrounded by stacks of papers and demos, his craggy face lined with concern. "You're the only family I have left, Elaine. I couldn't bear to lose you, too."

"Thad," she said, "when I do decide to sell Dad's songs, I want you to be the agent."

"Thanks, Elaine. But that's another topic. One we need to discuss. I'm thinking you may have been right to be cautious. Some suspicious things are going on with CMP."

"Why do you say that?"

"Lisa called and insisted that I come to her office. While I was there, she raised the offer for the collection. She said they would be willing to up the advance by thirty thousand. They want this deal so badly that I can't help but think there's a reason. They might know more about the demand for Uncle Steven's work than I do."

Elaine didn't reply.

"Still, it's your decision," Thad said. "If you decide to sell Uncle Steven's songs, you'll have plenty of money. You wouldn't need to stay with the tour."

"I wouldn't think of quitting now. I intend to be at Club Paradise tomorrow for their grand opening."

* * * *

Early the next morning Elaine stopped by the hotel desk.

"Has Derrick Kline checked in yet?"

The girl looked on the computer before replying, "Yes, late Wednesday evening."

So Derrick had caught up with the tour. Probably he arrived just in time to see her leave for her date with Rex. That would be the only explanation for his not calling her.

"Would you ring his room for me?"

The girl automatically pressed buttons on the desk phone. After a while she replied. "There's no answer."

Since he was staying at the Sea Breeze, finding him would pose no problem. Elaine looked into the café, then stepped out on the vast patio lined with umbrellas, deck chairs, and rows of tables. The after-effects of last night's storm lingered. The dreary fog that covered the sky was reflected in the rolling gray waves of the ocean.

She spotted Derrick at once. He wandered aimlessly along the shore. He wore a jeans jacket, his lean frame hunched against the morning chill. The familiar sight of him, looking so solitary and sad, for a moment made her heart lurch.

Part of her wanted to see him, after all, he had been her friend for many years. Their little co-authoring team had survived both failure and success, and these things she would not forget. Yet another part of her wished she did not have to face him here today.

Derrick slumped down on the rocks of a jetty. He reached into his pocket and unwrapped a breakfast roll. Absently, he tossed bits of it to the gulls.

He did not look at her as she approached and took a seat beside him.

"I talked to Thad," she said. "He told me you were here."

Elaine's voice faded leaving only the cries of the gulls, the frantic flapping of wings as they vied over the scraps of bread.

"I came to battle the windmills," Derrick said.

Despite herself, Elaine laughed. For a moment, he came back into focus as the old Derrick, the "big brother" she had never had. Like a brother, he had teased and bullied her, showed protectiveness and scorn.

"You shouldn't be here Derrick. Why are you?"

"I think you know, Elaine," he replied, staring out at the waves. "I've come to take you back to New Orleans."

If Derrick were in love with her, he would not be seeing another woman as he had admitted to doing. "We've already discussed that. Nothing's changed."

He turned to her in that slow, lazy way, smiling a little. "Elaine, I guess I rushed you too much with all that talk of marrying me. I'm perfectly content to go back to the way things were before."

"Why do you think there's been such a change?" Elaine asked. "We can still write our songs together. We can still be what we've always been, good friends."

Derrick's voice no longer sounded slow or languid. "You're on the way, Elaine. You can make it to the top without the help of Rex Tobin."

Derrick rose, drawing her to her feet, too. "You and I can sing together. I'm just as good as he is. We'll record 'The Glitter of the Road,' and it will be a hit! We'll do your father's songs, too! You just don't need Tobin anymore, Elaine!"

She gazed at him, shocked by her own thoughts, seeing characteristics she associated with Denny Mack—contempt for those who succeed, ugly jealousy over the spotlight. Derrick, opportunist—looking out for his own interests, not hers.

No, this couldn't be right. Derrick was only trying in his way, which was not always smooth or tactful, to protect her.

The gulls began sparring in earnest, fighting as if it were a matter of life or death over the bits of bread. Elaine felt her life was in the same kind of turmoil, with everyone she knew vying for control.

"It used to be you and me. I'm not going to let Tobin take you away from me!" His large, hazel eyes became pleading. "You've just got to come back with me!"

"I've told you before, Derrick, I'm not going to do that."

"You're so blind, Elaine," Derrick said acidly. "The only reason Rex Tobin hired you was to steal you away from me. Then he'll dump you, just like he did Lisa Craft."

* * * *

Elaine broke free of Derrick's grasp and started back to the hotel. He made no attempt to catch up with her, just lagged behind. She could feel his eyes on her, feel the ever-growing sullenness of his mood.

She cut toward the side-entrance to the hotel and crossed the garden area where she had run through the rain last night. Elaine heard Derrick call her name before she reached the door.

"Elaine. Wait!"

He moved rapidly now, stopping a few feet from her.

"You're not going to cut me out now. You're going straight to the top, and I'm going to be the one there with you!"

He grabbed her arm roughly. "I'm going back to New Orleans, and you're coming with me!"

"I'd suggest," a deep voice spoke up, "that you go back to New Orleans alone. The sooner the better."

Rex must have come from the annex. He strode from the tree-lined pool toward them and halted, face to face with Derrick.

Elaine saw Derrick tense. For a moment she was afraid he was going to hit Rex. Rex thought so, too, for his fist clenched at his side as he waited for Derrick to make the first move.

"No, Derrick. Please don't start a fight."

Her words caused Derrick to turn toward her. "I want an answer, once and for all. Are you going to go back with me or stay with him?"

"I'm going to do just what I told you before. I'm going to finish this tour."

Derrick whirled back to Rex, who remained in guarded stance.

"You heard what she said," Rex spoke calmly, but with warning. "If you don't want to run into real trouble, you just leave Elaine alone."

"You scare me!" Derrick said in a spiteful, schoolboy way. As he spoke, he advanced a step. "You're not going to win, Big Shot," he said. "Just remember, I'm going to be right here watching every move you make!"

CHAPTER TWENTY

A tap sounded on Elaine's door. Thinking Derrick had followed her, she swung it open, ready with words of dismissal.

Rex, blue eyes steady and emotionless, black hair, damp and ruffled from the ocean breeze, regarded her solemnly. He did not reach for her. He did not speak.

Elaine, reacting in the same formal manner, stepped back and admitted him into the room.

"Oscar got the report back from the car rental company," he said, his voice as distant as his eyes. "The failed brakes could not have been an accident."

Elaine glanced away from him, toward the balcony where she had seen the car with lifted hood. A black outline of Stetson hat, a glint of silver band, flashed before her eyes. Rex stepped toward her, extending a white envelope. Without looking inside, Elaine knew what it must contain—a plane ticket back to New Orleans.

"You can't break our contract," she said, her eyes locking on his.

"I can," Rex replied, "and I have. Under no circumstances will you be allowed to finish this tour."

"I want to stay. I want to sing on tomorrow night's show."

Elaine thought she read in his eyes a flicker of hesitation, a moment of doubt or regret.

"That's not possible."

Even though she already knew about Lisa's taking her place, she still said, "My absence will leave an unfilled slot."

Avoiding her gaze, Rex said. "I've already arranged for your replacement."

She had been prepared and hadn't expected to react at all, but she did. She felt stung by the image of Lisa Craft singing with Rex, completing the job that had been assigned to her.

"I thought Lisa had refused to appear."

"The company is part hers. She has agreed to assume responsibility by finishing the tour."

Elaine stared at him, aghast. Rex and Lisa had to be working together, or else he would not deliberately put Lisa in danger. Not unless Lisa was to be eliminated, too. She started to challenge him, to tell him about what she had seen from this very balcony, but could not bring herself to voice the words. She merely averted her gaze, wanting to keep her ever-growing doubts of him a secret. Her hand clenched around the envelope he had given her. Yes, she had a ticket, but that didn't mean she would ever reach New Orleans alive.

"Why don't you pack your belongings," Rex said, his words suddenly conciliatory. "First thing tomorrow, I'll drive you to the airport."

"No need to bother," Elaine replied stiffly. "I'll take a cab."

* * * *

After an uneasy night, Elaine rose early. Saturday, the day of the show—she was filled with horror as if she were once again behind the wheel of an out-of-control car. She had not even glanced at the envelope Rex had given her. It didn't matter what time the flight left. She had no intention of being on it. Elaine didn't know what she was going to do, but she did know that disaster loomed just ahead—for someone—and she had only a matter of hours left to avert it.

The shrill ringing of the phone broke through her thoughts. The caller couldn't be Rex. He and the Wind River Band had left the hotel some time ago for their scheduled rehearsal at The Paradise Club in downtown Corpus Christi.

She allowed the phone to ring several times, then cautiously lifted the receiver.

"Hello."

No dial tone sounded, just an over-powering quietness, as if someone had invaded her privacy only to listen.

"This is Elaine Sands."

A voice, very low and hollow, spoke only one word, "Tonight."

The word resounded into the stillness, making her feel

as if she were staring into a dangerous, whirling abyss.

"Derrick."

She didn't know why she spoke Derrick's name, for she didn't even suspect that he was the one on the other end of the line. The caller made no response. He merely hung up, the click, a stealthy sound, as still and muffled as the voice had been.

No doubt the call had been made from one of the many pay phones around the hotel. Trying to trace it would be futile.

* * * *

Lisa Craft arrived at the Sea Breeze Hotel with her usual flurry. Her glossy black hair and sequined dress rippled as she passed her fast-gathering fans, smiling at one, waving at another. She paused to talk to Derrick, who sat alone at a patio table, nursing a cup of coffee.

Elaine watched from the lobby as the two of them talked and laughed like old friends. Derrick's large hazel eyes remained on Lisa as she continued on to the reception area. Elaine intercepted her as she reached the desk.

"Lisa. Is there somewhere we can talk?"

Lisa glanced at her watch. "Actually, I don't have much time. My flight was delayed, and I was expected at the club several hours ago."

"This is important."

"Then we'll talk. On the way up to my room." Lisa picked up her key and turned to a straggling of fans that had trailed after her. "Don't miss our show tonight at Club Paradise," she called. "The best ever."

Once in the elevator, Lisa's smile faded and she said almost crossly, "What is it that you want?"

"I thought I should tell you, I received another phone call today."

The natural flush drained from Lisa's face. "Was it a threat? What did he say?"

"Just one word—tonight "

"I'm scared enough without your adding to my worries," Lisa said almost as if she resented Elaine's attempt to warn her.

"You don't have to go on," Elaine stated.

"You're wrong there. Rex forced my hand. He said if I didn't go on tonight, he wouldn't either."

Lisa remained sullenly silent for a moment, then added, "Then where would that leave Craft Music Productions? Club Paradise is huge and influential. They've been planning the grand opening of their new building for six months and doing constant promotions. Under these conditions, how can I not show up?"

"I want to sing tonight," Elaine said. "I'll take your place."

Lisa gave her a long, cool look. "You just don't get it, do you? It's not you they want to hear, Elaine. It's me. Rex and me."

The elevator stopped at the fifth floor, but no one got on. Lisa irritably pushed the button again.

"How did the audit turn out?" Elaine asked.

"Just how I suspected," Lisa answered shortly. "But they are still working on the final results."

When they reached the twelfth landing, Lisa said, "Just don't worry about our problems, Elaine. And stay away from the show. This is not your concern."

* * * *

Hours passed with relentless swiftness. Elaine had plenty of time to think. Certain events did not fit in to any conclusion she drew. First, the attempt on Denny Mack's life seemed an excessive build-up for tonight, if that's what it had been. Second, if Rex wanted her out of the way, why wouldn't he simply arrange for another accident at the show instead of supplying her with an airplane ticket and insisting she stay away? Because she wanted Rex to be innocent so badly, she was tempted to believe that he was doing all he could to protect her.

As the time for the show approached, Elaine made a snap decision. She was going to take a cab to Club Paradise. She had no idea what she could do once she arrived at the performance, but, one thing was certain, she couldn't force herself to remain at the hotel. As she changed clothes, she felt the heaviness of approaching disaster.

She moved numbly to the balcony and looked toward the sea. The height of her room, twelve floors up, caused the scene below to look distant and unreal. As her gaze swept over the parking lot, to her surprise she spotted the tour bus. The lettering, Rex Tobin and the Wind River Band, was barely distinguishable in the dusky mist.

A man, just leaving the hotel, was heading toward the bus. She could see his straight frame, his dark, western suit, his smooth, silverish hair. Elaine watched as Levi reached the driver's seat, then, as if just remembering some forgotten chore, he stopped, and hurried back toward the entrance.

Why had Levi returned so close to the time the show was to begin? For a moment Elaine felt gripped with suspicion. Levi, always silently working behind the scenes, accountant, more than singer. Money—wasn't that the usual motive for murder? Whatever was going on must surely center on Craft Music Productions and the millions of dollars at stake.

A possibility existed that neither Lisa nor Rex was involved. Oscar had said that both Lisa and Rex went through Levi to spend company money. Even though Lisa was the one who had ordered a special audit, that didn't mean Rex and Levi were working together. Levi could be mishandling Craft Music Production funds on his own. Such things happened every day, the good and trusted employee deciding to cash in at the firm's expense.

Levi always kept his briefcase close at hand. It must be on the bus right now. Elaine caught the elevator down to the ground floor and hurried toward the bus. She didn't have time to study the contents of the briefcase now. She must act fast, slip into the bus and take the briefcase.

Using the key she had not yet returned, Elaine entered the bus. The dark drapes had been drawn, which left the interior in semi-darkness. She opened the closet where she had often seen Levi store his belongings and anxiously drew out the bulging, leather briefcase. Unable to resist the impulse, she opened it with nervous fingers. Even if she couldn't tell anything about the bookkeeping, she might find some other clue, some evidence that Levi had printed the warning note she had found on her door in Houston.

Neat stacks of papers, many clipped together and carefully labeled, lay inside. Elaine lifted them one at a time, scanning numbers, reading notations. Had she actually expected his guilt to be recorded in the row after row of careful figures?

All she was going to find here were meaningless numbers, numbers that meant nothing without hours of auditing. She lifted the black ledger Levi often wrote in while on the bus. She had no time to study this now. She would take it with her to her room.

Before Elaine could close the briefcase, a sudden noise sounded. She whirled around, face to face with Levi Culver! She stood frozen as Levi stepped inside, the bus door swinging shut behind him. His form became rigidly straight; his eyes, shielded behind dark-tinted glasses, focused on the briefcase.

He did not speak at once. When he did, it was only to say quietly, "You startled me, Elaine. Rex told me you had left for New Orleans."

He stepped forward, calmly retrieving the briefcase, allowing it to hang loosely at his side. His closeness gave her a clear view of his eyes, steady and hard, behind the dark lenses.

"It's almost time for the show to start," Elaine said.

"In less than an hour," he replied. "The manager wanted me to return the contract he gave me to look over, but I found I had left it in my room. What are you doing out here?"

"Looking for one of my notebooks."

Levi's gaze fell again to his briefcase. "Did you think you were going to find it in here?" He remained staring at her as if uncertain of what he should do next.

Elaine's breath stopped. He stood between her and the door. He might decide not to allow her to leave here. But surely he wouldn't harm her, not here, not now.

"I'm going back to the club," Levi said at last, his hand tightening on the handle of the briefcase. "Can I give you a ride somewhere? The airport?"

"No, thanks."

He made no move to leave. Fear gripped her. Levi now knew that she suspected him, and what that meant, she could only guess. Elaine started to the door and Levi stepped aside, but as she reached for the handle, he called her back.

"Elaine." Alertness, perceptiveness showed on his aristocratic features. "If you're worried about my bookkeeping," he said slowly, "Lisa had a complete audit done right before we left on this tour. Everything was found perfectly intact."

Elaine watched the bus join the heavy traffic that led toward the bridge. She felt more certain than before that the murder attempts had been directed solely at Rex and centered on the millions involved in Craft Music Productions. She now possessed a clear fact: either Lisa Craft or Levi Culver was lying to her.

CHAPTER TWENTY-ONE

If Elaine believed Levi, Denny Mack had not returned to New Orleans to instigate an audit of company funds. In fact, Denny Mack would not have been in New Orleans, but here, the man Elaine had seen tampering with the rental car. Lisa could have made up the story of his being in New Orleans, maybe even sending someone else here with a flight ticket, so Denny would have an established alibi when the "accident" was determined to be murder.

It would follow then, that Denny Mack was the man Lisa had been secretly seeing all along, the reason Rex and Lisa had broken up. It suddenly occurred to Elaine that Lisa, not one of Denny's fans, had been the woman drinking wine with him on the bus in Houston.

If that were so, then Denny, afraid that Elaine was getting too close to the truth, had staged the accident for himself, which he tried to blame on to Oscar. He had insisted that it be reported to the sheriff, whose record would state that Denny Mack had been a target of the killer, too.

With Rex eliminated, Denny would become Lisa's

business partner and the two of them would take full control of Craft Music Productions.

Logical, yes, but how was Elaine ever going to prove it?

She felt certain now that she had been right all along—Rex, not she, was in danger! Since Denny's plan to kill Rex in the car accident had failed, he was certain to strike again tonight.

* * * *

With pounding heart, Elaine took the elevator up to the twelfth floor where all of the tour members were staying. The long corridor seemed totally deserted. Elaine lingered outside her door. She hadn't decided exactly what she was going to do, not until she spotted a maid pushing a cart into an adjoining corridor. Elaine hurried toward her.

"Excuse me," she said. "I seem to have locked my keys in the room."

Taking Elaine's uneasiness for embarrassment, the woman flashed her a kindly smile.

"Don't worry. Happens all the time. Which room is yours?"

"This one, 1207."

Elaine breathed a sigh of relief as the maid unlocked the door to Denny Mack's room. She closed the door behind her, leaning against it for a moment. What did she expect to find in Denny's room? An airplane ticket proving he had been in New Orleans? Some letter or correspondence from Lisa that would link them together as lovers?

Elaine, feeling like a criminal, began making a

methodic search. She looked through every drawer, most of them stuffed with bright, expensive clothing. She checked the closet, examining pockets of trousers and jackets.

At last she drew out Denny's large, leather suitcase. The emptiness inside left her discouraged.

She had started to close the case when she noticed a slight bulge in one of the side pockets. Inside she found an unmarked cassette. She glanced around for a tape player. She remembered the portable one she had brought from home, which was in her own room. She would take the tape with her.

Elaine left the door slightly ajar thinking she would return the cassette after she had listened to it. Inside her room she rushed over to the small tape player, inserted Denny's tape, and pressed the button. The room was filled with Denny Mack's high, rich voice. He was singing the haunting lyrics to her father's song, "Silver Bayou Dreamer."

She pressed fast-forward. Denny had made a demo of S.S. Sands entire collection. What could that mean?

"Do you like it?"

Elaine turned, startled. In her haste she must not have completely closed the door. Denny stepped through it, smiling broadly. Once inside, Denny stopped and raised a hand to slide back the black Stetson he wore. Elaine's eyes locked with horror upon the hat, upon the wide, silver band that glinted with his quick movement.

The scene at the Delta Hotel gift shop flashed through her mind. Levi had been so annoyed at Denny for copying everyone else's purchases. That morning Denny must have bought a hat with a silver band exactly like Rex's! Elaine knew now without a doubt the man she had seen in the shadows leaning over the Toyota had been Denny Mack!

Her heart seemed to stop. What was he doing here? Why wasn't he at the rehearsal with the others?

Denny's big smile faded. His features, without it, looked threatening, ominous. His sturdy, muscular frame towered in front of her, blocking the door, which was now firmly closed. Elaine was left with no means of escape. Denny stepped menacingly closer.

Elaine forced herself to remain where she was, to say with steady voice, "What are you doing with my father's songs?"

"It's Lisa's idea," he said, almost smugly.

Reaching over, he deliberately turned up the cassette, speaking over the volume of his own recorded voice.

"And it's going to work!"

Lisa's plan was to become sole owner of Craft Music Productions. Elaine remembered Levi telling her that Lisa was an extravagant spender. Lisa, having squandered Bill Craft's personal fortune, the money she could get her hands on, now needed access to free spending of company funds. But Rex Tobin stood in the way. Lisa would not be able to continue her luxurious lifestyle unless she eliminated Rex!

Lisa Craft and no doubt a partnership in Craft Music Productions were Denny's motives for going to such extremes to kill Rex. Already filled with jealousy over Rex's success, he must have jumped at Lisa's suggestion that they murder her business partner so they could own and operate the company themselves.

Lisa had lied to Elaine about having received threatening phone calls. Lisa had put Denny up to making the calls, to writing the note. Since they planned to kill Rex, they needed to have a witness that some madman was out to seek revenge on the entire company!

“You faked the fall at the canyon,” Elaine said.

A hoot escaped his lips. “Look at me? Do you actually think I needed your help getting back to the top? I eased myself down the cliff to that branch and yelled. Convincing, wasn’t it? I even fooled the mighty Rex Tobin. And now it’s on record that the killer was after me as well as you and Rex.”

“You rigged the electrical wiring that night expecting to kill Rex,” Elaine said.

“Yes!” he answered. “But the car 'accident' I intended for both of you!”

He was standing close to her now. His face with the rough, red-stubble beard appeared hard and lined as he stared down at her.

“Eliminating Rex was all Lisa cared about. But not me. I have my own plans! Plans that concern those unrecorded songs of your father's!”

With Elaine out of the way, the rights to S.S. Sands' songs would revert to Thad, her only living relative, who would lose no time cutting the best deal. Denny, so egotistical, so desperate to be a star, had taken matters into his own hands, was working toward his own goal of becoming CMP's top recording star! Denny Mack, replacing the famous Rex Tobin, becoming with the help of S.S. Sands' finest work, a living legend!

Denny's glance darted toward the open door to the balcony.

"Rex will meet with an accident tonight. I had almost decided to let you live, but now I can't do that."

His words, spoken so cold-bloodedly, caused a chill to run though Elaine.

"Two deaths? How are you going to get away with that?"

"Lisa will say I was in New Orleans when the brakes were tampered with. And the guilty one couldn't have been Lisa. She was the first person to report to the police that she had received the threatening phone calls. The other tour members will support our stories. The police will say Rex and you were murdered by some deranged follower intent on destroying the show. The elusive killer will never be found! The same killer who entered your room and pushed you over the balcony to your death!"

With a sudden movement, Denny's strong hands locked on her shoulders. Elaine felt herself being dragged toward the open balcony doors. She struggled trying to escape the steel-like grip, but she knew it would be impossible to break away!

Music rang in her ears, Denny's voice singing her father's songs...the last words she would ever hear!

At that moment Elaine caught a movement at the entrance to her room, the slow turning of the brass handle, the door being opened very slowly. Elaine, unable to believe her eyes, caught a blurred glimpse of Rex stepping into the room.

In spite of all she could do, Denny was drawing her steadily closer to the edge of the balcony. Rex had reached the stand near the bed. He lifted a small, brass lamp from the table.

Elaine desperately struggled to free herself. For a moment Denny seemed to hesitate, his grasp on her loosening a little. Had he sensed Rex's presence? Elaine's thoughts whirled. She could not allow him to see Rex! She must think of some way to distract him.

"Denny, you don't have to kill me!" she gasped. "I'm perfectly willing to sign over my father's songs to you!"

She tried to pull away again, but he held her fast.

"I was only instructing Thad to hold out for more money. I will, Denny, I'll sign the contract."

In answer Denny's hands clamped angrily on her wrists. "It's way too late for that! Now I have to kill you because you know too much!"

Rex slowly crept up behind him.

"No, Denny, I won't talk! I won't tell anyone!"

"I can't take that chance, can I?"

He hurled her against the railing. Elaine could feel the cold metal bars striking her back.

"There's no other way! You have to die!"

At that instant, Rex struck the side of Denny's head. Denny staggered forward and reeled back before he hit the floor. Rex took a step forward, reached out for her, and

Elaine found herself gathered safely in his arms.

"Rex. How did you know where to find me?"

"You have Levi to thank for that. He told me you were still here. Then when Denny was missing from the practice too, I asked Shelby about him. Shelby told me Denny had asked him to cover for him until he returned. After that, I lost no time. I got Sam at the desk to give me the keys to both your room and Denny's. When I reached the corridor, I could hear the music."

"You must have known Denny Mack was behind this all along."

"Unfortunately, I didn't. I did know beyond any doubt that Lisa was behind the whole operation, but I didn't know who was working with her. I must admit I thought of Derrick, and even of your cousin, Thad. It wasn't until Shelby told me Denny Mack never left on the plane for New Orleans that I realized that Denny had never been a target at all, that he had rigged the attempt on his life and pretended to return to New Orleans so he would never be considered as a suspect. At first I believed they were after no one but me, but I kept thinking of your father's songs and I knew you were in danger, too. I wanted nothing more than to get you safely away from the show."

A gentle hand smoothed her hair, pressed her face closer against his chest. "But you're safe now. It's all over now, darling."

* * * *

The rehearsal was ending by the time Rex and Elaine reached the Paradise Club. The music stopped just as they entered the hall, and Lisa, a satisfied expression on her face, quickly left her position at the microphone and started down the aisle toward them.

"Where's Denny? Did you find him?" Her gaze shifted from Rex to Elaine and with the same bright, false manner, asked, "What are you still doing here? I thought you left for New Orleans."

"Not quite yet," Elaine replied. "I had some unfinished business to take care of."

When Lisa saw the two policemen making their way toward her, the smile drained from her face.

"Miss Craft, we'd like to have a word with you."

Lisa's eyes widened. "What is this all about?"

One of them began to read Lisa her rights while the other cuffed her hands behind her back. "Rex, stop them! Rex, can't you do something!"

Rex shook his head in reply.

Lisa's shrill voice echoed as she was led away. "I demand to speak to my lawyer!"

* * * *

The tour had gone full circle. Despite being short one band member, San Antonio had been a grand success. The last show scheduled at a huge club in New Orleans played to a full house. Elaine stood on the wing near the folds of curtain and listened to the bursts of laughter that followed Oscar's jokes.

Shelby would perform next. He had been so elated right before the show when Rex had told him he could fill in for Denny Mack. Elaine felt a sense of uneasiness as the boy took his place in front of the microphone, but once he began singing, the feeling changed to relief. She had not known the boy possessed such talent.

"You did a fine job tonight, Shelby," Rex said after the autographs had been signed and the last of the fans had left. "I'm willing to make your position permanent."

Shelby raised his head quickly. The sudden movement caused his long hair to swirl. Usually this motion revealed an attitude of defiance, but tonight he grinned and burst out, "A deal!"

"I talked to the police this morning," Levi remarked. "Denny Mack has made a full confession. It's going to be a very long time before he gets out of prison. Of course, Denny blamed Lisa for coming up with the idea and hounding him to carry it out."

"Lisa didn't understand the real Denny Mack," Oscar drawled. "The fact that once Denny's caught, Lisa goes down, too."

CHAPTER TWENTY-TWO

Elaine stopped outside Craft Music Production's towering building, breathing deeply of the brisk autumn air. The last time she had passed through these doors had been to enter the huge auditorium to audition for the tour. So much had happened since then. Lisa and Denny had been charged with two counts of attempted first-degree murder, Lisa had sold her share of the company to Oscar and Levi. Today Rex and Elaine were scheduled to record her song, "The Glitter of the Road."

Elaine, waiting for Rex, paused to admire the oil painting of her father, S. S. Sands. Rex had commissioned a friend of his to paint it from one of her father's favorite photographs. Rex had himself hung it beside the door leading into the auditorium.

Elaine sensed Rex's presence beside her.

"The studio is on the third floor."

Upstairs they ran across Oscar and Levi, who stood in front of the long line of offices, talking.

"I'm contemplating my name-plate," Oscar told them, a sparkle appearing in his eye.

"What do you think, Elaine? Big Oscar or Macho Macy?"

"Let's go with Oscar Macy, Partner," Levi said, "so your name plate will match mine."

Laughing, Rex and Elaine entered Rex's office. Through the glass wall she could see the recording studio, a small room with control panels containing a maze of dials, and beyond that, the glass encased room where they would sing together.

"Thad called this morning," Rex was saying. "We're going to meet tomorrow and sign the contract for your father's songs."

"I'm so glad that you'll be the one singing them!"

Rex's blue eyes met hers, lighting in that special way. It made her think of the first time she had really gazed into Rex's eyes. Now, as then, she was filled with a breathless joy.

Rex's arm encircled her. As he drew her close, Elaine thought of the final line to the song they were getting ready to record—*And we will have each other, And the glitter of the road.*

ABOUT THE AUTHORS

Loretta Jackson, former teacher of English and Creative Writing, lives in Junction City, Kansas. She and her sister, Vickie Britton, are co-authors of the "Ardis Cole Mystery" Series, novels set in exotic locations around the world. The sisters' research has recently taken them to Peru, Russia, Egypt, and China. Among their titles, generally of mystery and suspense, are NIGHTMARE IN MOROCCO, KILLER OF EAGLES, and MEXICAN MYSTIQUE, just released in Scotland and Italy.

Vickie Britton lives in the beautiful mountain town of Laramie, Wyoming, with her husband, Roger. They own and operate a local computer store. Their son, Ed, is a student at the Colorado Institute of Art in Denver, where he is studying graphic art and animation. Vickie has co-authored with her sister, Loretta Jackson, over thirty novels. They also enjoy writing short stories and have two new collections from Whiskey Creek Press, a mainstream anthology, NO LONGER DRIFTING, and a collection of suspense stories, THE BLOODY KNIFE.

For your reading pleasure, we welcome you to visit our web bookstore